Publicity Girl

Publicity Girl

by Robin McKown

G. P. Putnam's Sons — New York

© 1959 by Robin McKown

Library of Congress Catalog Card Number: 59-5225
Manufactured in the United States of America
Published simultaneously in the Dominion of Canada
by Longmans, Green and Co., Toronto

jM219pw

ACKNOWLEDGMENTS

For the advice and help I needed in lending veracity to Edwina's story, I would like to express my special appreciation to public relations counsel Jerry Sherman; book publicist Benn Hall; E. C. Wood of the Eastern Greyhound Lines publicity department; Robert B. Stewart of the Procter & Gamble Company public relations department; Paul Jones of the National Safety Council; Miss Elizabeth Reese of Raymond Loewy; Miss Eleanor Phillips and Miss Adele Gilruth of Stephen Fitzgerald and Company; to Arthur Beckhard and Sherman Graff.

ROBIN McKOWN

For Clyde and Edith

Publicity Girl

Chapter 1

Above the receptionist's desk was a full-length painting of Abraham Lincoln. From where Edwina was sitting, he seemed to be staring with disdain at the lemon-colored drapes, the thick tufted beige rug, the turquoise upholstered sofa, and at the queer pale rose-colored statuary in the corner, a mass of cubes and curves set off by indirect lighting.

He doesn't belong in this ultramodern setting any more than I do, she told herself.

The receptionist, a very pretty, very young girl with platinum-blond hair, met her gaze and smiled.

"You're here about the secretary's position, aren't you?" she said in a distinctly Southern drawl. "You shouldn't have any trouble landing it, honey. Just act feminine. Mr. Pritchard likes women to be feminine." Complacently she took out an enormous compact and began powdering her nose with a downy puff.

"I did apply for a job as secretary," Edwina admitted, "but I don't really want it. That is, I want a job where I can write. I've had some newspaper experience. Of course,

I'd be willing to do anything for a while until I learn my way around."

"For pity's sake, don't tell him that." The receptionist closed her compact with a little click. "If there's one thing he can't stand, it's a publicity woman. He thinks women should be decorative"—she paused to pat her hair in place —"but that they should know their place in an office and not try to compete with men in a man's world." The last words had a parrotlike quality.

Edwina opened her mouth to say that a man had no right in this day and age to say what women could and could not do, but was saved this waste of breath when the monitor switchboard buzzed. "Robert Pritchard and Associates," the receptionist said sweetly, as she picked up her phone. "May I help you?"

The call was a personal one and as she chatted on, Edwina became more and more restless. She assured herself she wasn't nervous, just cold. Her square-necked pale-blue dress was designed to combat the mid-July heat outside, not for sitting immobile in the chill air-conditioned reception room. She cast her eyes up toward Abraham Lincoln to transmit a message to him: Next time I come here, remind me to bring my mink.

If she had guessed what it would be like to look for a job in New York she might have thought twice before leaving Dantonville. For a month she had been making the rounds without a nibble. She shuddered inwardly, remembering the daily ordeal: doing her blond hair up on top of her head instead of in the ponytail she wore at home; washing and ironing one of her cotton dresses each night so it would be fresh for morning; seeing that pumps, gloves and bag were spotlessly white; using a touch of

12

lipstick which she had never bothered with even at the university except for dances; and always going out in the morning fresh and confident—and returning in the evening limp and wilted and footsore.

At the beginning she had gone to the newspapers, sure that she would qualify as a cub reporter. The men there had been friendly enough but none had given her encouragement.

"If we hired every youngster who edited his college paper, we'd all have to move out," a veteran city desk editor had told her. That her father ran a weekly newspaper and that even in grade school she had helped him set type and run the press (later on handling local news and in general serving as his star reporter) didn't seem to do her any good here.

Unlike others of her classmates, she had not jumped right out of college into New York. There had been a year working for Judge Nordstrom in her home town after graduation, to save up a little money, and, as her father put it, to have time to mature. The way he said it made her feel rather like a peach taken off the tree too soon and left in the sun to ripen for eating. Still, in principle he had been all for her dream of making a career in the Big City.

"There's no future here," he said, as he had so often said before. "Look what's happened to me."

"Nothing bad has happened to you except you're not rich," she chided him. "You're your own boss, you keep your own hours, and everyone in town loves you. You have a wonderful life."

He admitted there was a grain of truth in what she said but still advised her to get away while she could.

With her mother it was different. Her mother's pleasure

was in washing her linens to a dazzling whiteness, in keeping her house so that one could quite literally and quite comfortably eat from the floors, and in preparing for her husband the Norwegian dishes he had grown to like. She had little formal education and was overwhelmed that her oldest daughter was a university graduate and that the younger, Doris, would have the same opportunity. But she was unhappy at the idea of Edwina's leaving home before she was married. Only when her husband had written to his sister Margaret in New York and arranged for Edwina to stay with her had the mother become reconciled.

But none of the family, least of all Edwina, had suspected she would not be welcomed with open arms by all those New Yorkers responsible for giving out jobs. When the list of newspapers, big and little, was about exhausted, a personnel manager had suggested she try publicity. "There's much more opportunity in that field for a woman. Every product in the country needs publicity and a person to handle it. It pays well, too."

The idea had appealed to Edwina, who had started at once calling on the larger publicity agencies. But the personnel manager had been wrong; no one seemed to need her at all. With her funds almost gone, she had thought of a different approach. As a result she was sitting on the turquoise upholstered sofa waiting for an interview with the president of Robert Pritchard & Associates.

The receptionist, whose name according to the brass plaque on her desk was Miss Evarts, hung up when someone from inside buzzed her to get *Look* magazine on the phone. Then a blond young man with a self-satisfied air dashed out, pulling on a sport jacket. He stopped long

14

enough to ask Miss Evarts, whom he called "darling," if she would call his mother and tell her he wouldn't be able to make cocktails tonight as he was working late.

"Who are you kidding, Eric?" Miss Evarts demanded disrespectfully and ungrammatically, but she obliged him.

Right after that a girl with mouse-colored hair and a thin peaked face stopped at the desk to say she was going to the post office and could she bring back a coke for Miss Evarts—whom she called "Pat." "I'd love it, Anna, honey," Miss Evarts said.

Next a tall distinguished-looking man with horn-rimmed glasses and dark curly hair, about thirty-five or so Edwina judged, walked in and informed the receptionist that he was G. Harrison Dawes and that he had an appointment with Mr. Odell. Edwina noticed him particularly because he seemed to embody the characteristics attributed to successful Madison Avenue publicity men —at least in movies: poise, good looks and faultless attire. At any rate, something about him brought forth Miss Evarts' most gracious smile as she directed him to go right in, Mr. Odell's office was the second door to the left.

"I like that type of male, don't you?" Miss Evarts addressed Edwina. Without waiting for an answer, she rushed on, "Do you mind if I ask a personal question? Do you use rouge?"

"Why, no," Edwina said. "Why?"

"I've been wanting to ask you that but it seemed rather personal. I thought you had natural color but you don't see people with naturally pink cheeks up here in New York. Everybody is pasty."

"I used to play baseball on the boys' team at home when

15

I was a little girl," Edwina told her, laughing. "I guess it was good for my circulation."

"Is that how you did it?" Miss Evarts inquired, quite seriously. "I must remember that. I like the way you do your hair, too. Like Wallie Simpson, only her hair is dark. You've had a long wait, haven't you? It isn't fair to keep people waiting like that. Oh, here's Miss Dobbs now."

Miss Dobbs was a tall efficient-looking woman with auburn hair, classical features, and dressed in a tailored navy suit.

"Miss Fiske? I'm Mr. Pritchard's secretary. He will see you now," she said. She was not smiling.

A moment later Edwina was ushered into the spacious office of the head of Robert Pritchard & Associates. From behind a large blond-wood desk a short heavy-set man with dark hair plastered back from a high forehead rose and reached out his hand.

"How nice of you to stop by." His voice was loud, hearty and jovial. "Sit down. I want you to tell me about yourself. So you're from Illinois. You look Swedish. Don't they have a lot of Swedish settlers out in that part of the country? But Fiske isn't a Swedish name, is it?"

She was actually Norwegian-American, Edwina informed him as she sank into the comfort of a large blue-leather armchair. That is, her mother was the daughter of a Norwegian immigrant farmer. Her father was of English ancestry. He ran a newspaper in Dantonville where she had been brought up. She had mentioned that in her letter to him.

"So you did." He picked up the letter from a pile on his desk. "You went to the State University, worked summers

16

in your father's office, graduated as a major in journalism. Now that's fine. Knowing something about journalism should be a help to you here. . . ." He paused, glancing down at the letter. "You worked as a secretary to Judge Nordstrom of Dantonville for a year. That means you're okay on shorthand and typing."

He made it a statement rather than a question. In all honesty she felt she should point out that the judge was an old man and retired, and that being his secretary had meant going to his house every day, where he had dictated the memoirs he sometime hoped to get published. That thus, in spite of the shorthand and typing, she knew nothing of office procedure. But Mr. Pritchard didn't give her a chance.

"When can you start work, Miss Fiske?"

She gasped. "You mean I'm hired?"

"That's right." He continued in a crisp manner: "Miss Fiske, I pride myself I can judge character quickly. Your letter told me everything I needed to know. I only had to meet you to confirm my hunch you would fit in. Your salary will be seventy-five dollars a week. Raises are dependent on merit. Hours are nine to five, five days a week, and time and a half and dinner money for overtime. You will have the usual legal holidays, hospitalization, and so forth. You should count on starting Monday. I will take you in to meet Mr. Odell who handles our tea account and whose work you will be doing."

For a moment Edwina couldn't seem to move. The form letter she had sent to a dozen or so of the smaller publicity offices, stressing her knowledge of shorthand, had been a last resort. She really hadn't expected it to work. Yet now at her first interview she was being offered

17

a job at a salary she had hardly dared hope for. She felt dazed.

"What's the matter? Don't you want the job?" Mr. Pritchard was staring down at her.

"I want it very much," she told him firmly.

"Good."

He took her by the arm and marched her across the hall where he flung open the door. "Jeff, I want you to meet Miss Fiske, your new secretary," he boomed, and stopped short. "Sorry. Didn't know you had anybody with you."

"I'm just leaving, sir." The distinguished man who had come in while Edwina was waiting rose to his feet with an easy movement.

"Mr. Pritchard, Mr. Dawes. And Miss Fiske," said the gentleman behind the desk, who was white-haired, stoutish, with ruddy complexion, in his shirt sleeves and smoking a pipe.

"Delighted," said Mr. Dawes. "Mr. Pritchard, I've been wanting to meet you ever since I read the story in *Modern Decorator* last May about your new home." He turned to Edwina and bowed slightly. "Congratulations on your new job. I wish you luck with it." He shook hands with the man behind the desk. "I'll have the glossies messengered over to you in a day or so, Odell." Without any further fuss he was gone.

"Who is he?" Mr. Pritchard demanded, looking after him.

"G. Harrison Dawes," said Mr. Odell, "a partner of Madden and Dawes, an agency that sprang up about a year ago. He handles the New York baseball team, the Wings, whose trainer is strong on the boys drinking tea. He's going to send me some prints."

"A smart young man," Pritchard commented. "I wish some of you around here had his memory for faces and names and dates. I wish I did myself," he added, taking the sting out of his remark.

Edwina, momentarily forgotten, looked around. Mr. Odell's office was as different from the rest of the place as the nineteenth century from the twentieth. Currier and Ives prints lined one side of the room, above a Victorian sofa upholstered in rose damask. There were small hook rugs, a Chinese teakwood coffee table, a couple of Duncan Phyfe chairs, and a big old-fashioned carved mahogany desk, behind which her new boss sat on a homely swivel chair.

"I'll leave Miss Fiske with you," Mr. Pritchard said finally. "You can tell her something about her duties."

Mr. Odell swung himself around toward her when the company president had departed. "Your duties? I don't quite know what they are myself. You'll find out about them as you go along, no doubt. I suppose you know what publicity is?"

"I have a general idea."

"Publicity, like advertising," he explained, "is the art of making known to a certain public certain facts about a certain thing, person, product, company, or what-not. Unlike advertising, publicity space is not paid for, at least not in dollars and cents. Some people have the impression that publicity is the art of getting something for nothing. We prefer to consider ourselves unpaid servants of the press. That is, we provide news and information to our press friends which would take them a good deal of effort to get without us."

"I never thought of it like that," Edwina told him, "but

19

I can see what you mean. What kind of publicity do you do here?"

"I'm coming to that," he assured her, taking another puff on his pipe. "There are all sorts of publicity agents, of course. At one extreme there are press agents who are pleased to get a picture of a would-be starlet into a tabloid, or to have a Broadway columnist tell a joke attributed to one of their clients. At the other extreme are the public relation counselors, whose clients may include foreign governments looking for American tourist trade or top corporations seeking to build good will." He looked at her quizzically. "But you want to know what Pritchard does."

"I do very much." She sat quietly in one of the small chairs. His impersonal comments had had the effect of putting her at her ease. It was a relief not to have to talk about herself and her qualifications.

"We are a small office," Mr. Odell continued, "but the few accounts we handle are substantial ones. One of them is the Dorey Air Conditioner Corporation. Pritchard supervises that personally. Eric Kingston is account executive for the Golden Arrow Bus Lines. My responsibility is the Tea Conference Board, the aim of the campaign being to get Americans to drink more tea. We all try to help each other on each of the accounts. We only take accounts that interest us. Enthusiasm is the first asset of a good publicity man."

The blond young man whom Edwina had seen earlier poked his head in at the door. "Say, Jeff, I just had a lulu of an idea. Suppose we get Golden Arrow to serve tea to their passengers, free. Good will at less than half a cent a cup. Think the newspapers will go for it?"

"No," said Mr. Odell, "I definitely don't. Go have another brainstorm. On second thought, come on in and meet my new secretary, Miss Fiske. Miss Fiske, this is Eric Kingston. If you talk nicely to her, Eric, maybe she'll do some work for you occasionally—that is, if you ever do any."

"Beautiful," Eric announced, staring at her. "Never fear, I'll be nice to her. Bob certainly knows how to pick them."

Edwina felt a flash of annoyance. "Flattery isn't necessary, Mr. Kingston," she said coolly. "I'll work for you whenever Mr. Odell instructs me to."

Odell chuckled. "Pay heed, Eric lad. It looks as if we've found someone not susceptible to your charms."

"I was just trying to be friendly." The youth grimaced. "It seems I flopped." He left.

Edwina rose, feeling the interview was over. "Thank you very much for explaining things to me, Mr. Odell. I'll be in Monday."

The plain girl she had seen talking to Miss Evarts was at the reception desk when Edwina passed by. Though she was putting through a call for someone, she looked up and smiled shyly. It was a nice friendly smile that made her almost attractive.

As she headed on toward the elevator she met Pat Evarts carrying her make-up kit.

"I'm so glad you got the job, honey." She gave Edwina an anxious look. "I hope you didn't say anything to them about wanting to write publicity."

Edwina shook her head. "No, I took your advice and didn't mention it."

Chapter 2

"They're a friendly, informal office, Matt. Not at all the way you think they are when you first walk in and see all the modernistic furniture and the chi-chi. I think I'm going to like it there, even if I am only a secretary."

"That's fine." Matt unfolded his large white napkin and spread it squarely on his knees. "So long as you don't fall in love with your boss. All secretaries do, you know."

Edwina sighed. It was just the sort of remark she could have expected from Matt. "You don't have to worry about that," she said, playing up to him. "Mr. Odell is an old man with white hair. And Mr. Pritchard, who is the president, is almost bald and on the bombastic side."

The waiter brought the menus, which Matt laid aside as he usually did.

"Two steaks medium rare. Home fries and green peas," he ordered for them both.

They were having dinner at Thornton's, the 86th Street branch, in celebration of Edwina's new job. But it wasn't really much of a celebration since Matt always took her to Thornton's for dinner when they had a date—because, as he said, you knew what you were getting and the waiters understood English.

"You don't mean to tell me there aren't any eligible men in the office?" he continued his banter as the waiter went off, giving her his crooked boyish grin that the girls at the State University had found so enchanting.

Edwina shrugged. "Since you insist, there is one. Mr. Kingston. He looks younger than you do and he's quite good-looking. He was the one person I didn't like much."

"You'd better watch out," Matt counseled. "True love always starts with the two people involved detesting each other."

Matt made a feature of this sort of repartee, and usually Edwina didn't mind. Tonight it bored her.

"Oh, for goodness sake," she said. "Can't we talk about anything else?"

He looked so hurt that Edwina repented her outburst immediately. "I'm sorry, Matt. I didn't mean to sound off like that."

"That's all right," he said, a little distantly. "Coming from you I don't mind it." He broke a roll and spread it thickly with butter, and she knew in advance what was coming: "The thing about you, Edwina, is that you have class. Other girls are just girls."

She remembered how thrilled she had been the first time he had said it. They had been in the same sophomore English class. Already, big lumbering Matt was a football hero, belonged to the best fraternity on the campus, and was easily the most popular youth at State. She was an unknown, whom no sorority had rushed, with no friends but the girls in her boardinghouse. One day he had asked her to have a coke with him after class. And as she was

23

sipping it, he had said, "The thing about you, Edwina, is that you have class."

After that he had asked her to help him with his English theme; he needed to pass the course if he stayed on in college. She was sure that when she had performed this service for him, she would see no more of him. Instead he had continued to date her frequently. In her junior year she had been a reporter on the college paper and was editor-in-chief of it in her senior year, so that before they graduated the social difference between them had been leveled off. In fact, she had moved in the so-called intellectual circle who considered football heroes "bourgeois." Still, everyone on the campus took it for granted that they would get married, and so did Edwina.

"Tell me how your job's coming along, Matt," she prompted as the waiter produced their steaks.

Matt was a salesman for the Blanchard Service, an organization that handled tax and bookkeeping problems for small businessmen. Whenever conversation lagged between them, as it did frequently now that they were no longer in college, Edwina had discovered she could fill the gap by asking him about his job.

This time was no exception. Matt launched at once into an account of a new approach he had worked out to sell the Blanchard service. He had walked into a laundermat, asked to see the manager, and told him that he was there to talk to him about his taxes. "He thought I was an internal revenue agent so when I told him I wasn't there to collect more taxes he was so relieved he bought our service on the spot."

Edwina found the story intolerably dull. She knew it hadn't been easy for Matt to adjust to the commercial

24

world after being a college celebrity, but still it seemed to her he shouldn't get so worked up about it. She pictured herself sitting across the breakfast table from him year after year, three hundred and sixty-five days a year, and always he would be talking about the Blanchard Service.

The thought depressed her so much that she interrupted to tell him all over again how the president of Pritchard had talked to her just two minutes and then hired her, about the fine offices and the air conditioning, and about what glamorous people she was sure to meet there. As she stressed this latter point, an image flashed in her mind of the tall dignified man who had said to her, "I wish you luck in your new job," but this she didn't mention to Matt.

"What'll you have for dessert, Edwina?" His voice sounded unusually curt.

"I couldn't eat anything more, Matt. You order something for yourself."

"Let's go, then." He summoned the waiter and demanded the check.

Watching him, she realized with a start that he had been just as bored when she talked about Pritchard as she had been with his precious Blanchard Service. And yet two people who were going to get married ought to be vitally interested in whatever concerned each other. What was wrong?

As he walked her out onto the street, she thought back nostalgically to their dates at college, the prom dances when he stubbornly refused to let fraternity brothers cut in on them, the suppers at the College Inn, with all the girls looking at her enviously, the drives out into the country.

"Let's don't ever quarrel, Matt," she pleaded, putting her arm in his as they strolled down the street.

"Everybody quarrels sometime or other," he said. "It's human nature."

They went to a movie after that. Matt held her hand all through it and everything seemed all right between them again. But when she invited him up for a cup of coffee afterwards he refused.

"I'd be jumpy. Your aunt would be watching me every second to see what I would break this time."

His good-night kiss was the merest peck on the cheek.

If that's the way he wants it, it's all right with me, Edwina told herself as she put the key into the lock of the apartment door. But she felt mildly distressed.

Aunt Margaret was still up, stretched out on the chaise longue in the sitting room, a book in her hand. She was wearing her rose velvet dressing gown that set off her blue-tinted gray hair.

"I hope you weren't waiting up for me, Margaret." At her own request, Edwina never used the word "aunt" in addressing this sister of her father's.

"Of course not, my dear," Margaret assured her in her well-modulated voice from which every trace of a Midwestern twang had long since vanished. "I just got home a few minutes ago from Professor Angus Rankin's lecture at the Museum of Natural History. It was all about the nervous system of invertebrates—absolutely fascinating. I bought one of his books which he autographed for me personally. I'm reading it now."

The nervous system of invertebrates seemed of remote interest to Edwina at the moment, but by now she was used to Margaret's wide-ranged enthusiasms. Since Ed-

26

wina had been living with her, her aunt had in turn found "absolutely fascinating" an exhibition of pre-Columbian South American musical instruments, a motion picture shown at the Brooklyn Museum reconstructing medieval life from paintings and sculpture, a transplanted Japanese house at the Modern Museum, and an evening watching Haitian dancing at the Palm Gardens.

"Did you have a nice time?" Margaret asked, closing her book on a carved ivory paper knife, a gift from one of her women friends who had worked with the YWCA in China.

"Fine," Edwina said. "Matt and I had dinner at Thornton's and then went to a movie."

"What movie did you see?"

"Oh, what was it called? I forget. It was about a couple who married for convenience, to save the man's legacy or something, and found out in the end they loved each other after all. Ronald Raeburn was in it."

"I see." Her aunt looked disappointed. "Too bad you didn't go to the Thalia. They have two lovely films there this week, one in Italian and one in French."

"I couldn't have dragged Matt there with a team of horses," Edwina confessed with a short laugh. "He abhors foreign movies."

"Must you always do what he suggests?" Margaret demanded mildly. "I think you should learn to assert yourself a little, Edwina. After all, it's up to the woman to lead a man toward the finer things in life."

"Would you like a cup of chocolate, Margaret?" Edwina broke in to stop this turn of the conversation.

Glad to have a few moments alone, she vanished into the kitchen as soon as Margaret said chocolate was a

27

lovely idea. Margaret was too polite to say so openly, but Edwina knew she classified Matt as a "Philistine," just as the rather snobbish intelligentsia at State had thought him "bourgeois." Such attitudes made Edwina feel protective toward her boy friend.

As she poured milk into the enamel saucepan and turned the gas on low, she thought back on the evening shortly after her arrival in New York, when at Margaret's suggestion she had invited Matt to dinner.

Margaret had prepared curry from a special recipe given her by the chef at an Indian restaurant she frequented, but Matt had scarcely been able to swallow it, having no more taste for foreign foods than for foreign films. Margaret had tried to draw him out about which modern artists he preferred and what he thought of the poetry of William Butler Yeats, and Matt had reacted with definite malicious intent by talking about football. The evening had reached its climax when, as they sat drinking after-dinner tea, Matt had demonstrated a certain play a little too graphically and swept his delicate Limoges cup and saucer to the floor, where it shattered into a dozen pieces.

Edwina did not consider herself a highbrow like her aunt, but she had to admit there were a lot of interesting things in the world besides football and the Blanchard Service. She felt suddenly very much alone.

The milk was simmering to a boil. She poured it out into two china cups—not the Limoges ones—added chocolate and sugar, placed them on the hand-painted Dutch tray with two embroidered Philippine napkins (another gift from one of Margaret's women friends), and carried the tray into the sitting room.

"How nice, dear," Margaret commented, as Edwina placed her cup on the sandalwood table by the chaise longue. "It *is* companionable to have you here."

"I feel very lucky to be here," Edwina replied dutifully.

It was true. Not many girls coming to New York as she had done had such charming living quarters. Margaret's attractive apartment, which she had leased when rents were still low, was on Riverside Drive overlooking the Hudson. One of Margaret's enthusiasms was antiques, and the French Provincial in the sitting room and the Early American in the bedrooms were the results of her excursions to auctions and antique dealers. Still, living here seemed rather like living in a model room in a museum. The lamps were not made to read by nor the chairs to relax in. There were times when Edwina had a yearning for the shabby, lumpy living-room divan at home, where she could sprawl out with her books to her heart's content, munching cheese and crackers or potato chips, mindless of where the crumbs might fall.

Margaret worked as a minor executive for the Mattson Foundation, which gave grants for worthy causes. It was a well-paid job, providing month-long annual vacations during which Margaret took cruises through the Caribbean or plane trips to Mexico or Oregon or Bermuda or some other "absolutely fascinating" place.

"Are you going to marry Matt?" Margaret asked unexpectedly.

"Why yes, I suppose so. That is . . ." Edwina found herself unable to finish.

"I'm not advising you whether you should or shouldn't," Margaret assured her with unusual earnestness. "I don't feel that Matt is your intellectual equal, but that in itself isn't enough of a reason not to marry him."

Edwina looked at her in surprise. It was the last admission in the world she could have expected from her aunt who put such stock in things of the intellect.

"I have a friend, a lovely woman," Margaret continued, taking a tiny sip of her chocolate. "She came to New York to work and the first year she was here she made friends with the son of her Italian butcher. They went to Coney Island and to the Bronx Zoo, and she had a great deal of fun. But when she introduced him to some of her friends, they made fun of his bad English and his ignorance of art and literature. She felt ashamed of him after that and told him she couldn't see him any more. Later on she became quite successful and independent, but she often wondered if she hadn't missed something by sending the butcher's son away."

Margaret frequently told Edwina about things that happened to her friends, but it took no great intuition on Edwina's part to surmise that the woman in this case was her aunt—whether or not the man was a butcher's son. It was a shock to her. She had always thought of Margaret as typical of the successful career woman who had no need of a man in her life. It seemed she was human after all. In an unusual burst of affection, she went over and put her arms around her aunt in a good-night hug.

But that night before she fell asleep, her thoughts were not of Matt and marriage but about her job and how wonderful it would be to earn seventy-five dollars a week, and how very soon she intended to show her employers that she too could do publicity.

Chapter 3

"Twenty-seven, please," Edwina told the elevator man as they zoomed upward.

All the other passengers were released before she was. The man turned to her as they reached the final stop.

"Your first day, isn't it, miss?"

"How did you know?"

"I know everyone who works here." His voice conveyed professional pride. "You won't have to tell me what floor tomorrow."

"I think that's remarkable," she said, wanting to praise him. "There must be hundreds of people working here."

"I guess there are all right," he agreed, accepting her homage as only his due. "I don't know all their names but I know them by floors. I'll look at you tomorrow and I'll remember that you're twenty-seven."

She reflected that it gave her a feeling of belonging to be recognized, even if it was only as "twenty-seven."

The reception room of Robert Pritchard & Associates was empty when she entered, except for Abraham Lincoln and the mysterious statue in the corner. As she waited, uncertainly, the girl she had heard called Anna came in carrying a pitcher.

"Good morning. You're early. I'm always the one who gets here first. I was watering the plants, Mr. Pritchard's philodendron and Mr. Odell's ivy. My name is Anna Dombrowski. Yours is Edwina Fiske, isn't it?" She had a breathless jerky way of speaking.

"I'm happy to know you, Anna. I guess you know I'm starting work here."

"Yes, I'm glad you are. It is always interesting to have new faces in the office. One always wonders what's behind new faces, don't you think? I'll show you where your desk is."

She led the way down the corridor past the executive offices to a bare room which looked crowded with its three desks and gray-green filing cabinets. A water cooler stood in one corner, a hatrack in another.

"It isn't as pretty here as it is up front, is it?" asked Anna. "But then, nobody comes back here. That is, nobody of importance. My desk is the one by the window. That doesn't seem fair, does it? But if I leave, you'll get my desk. That's the way Dorothea Dobbs says it should be. Your desk is this one facing mine. The other desk is for anybody—the accountant when he comes, or if we get temporary help. Shall I show you how to open up your typewriter?"

Without waiting for an answer she showed how easy it was to raise the top of the desk so that the typewriter slid into place.

"What a beauty it is!" exclaimed Edwina. She admired the multiple gadgets, the gray casing, the rubber-covered keys, comparing it wistfully to the ancient model in her father's newspaper office. A fine typewriter should have many fine words in it, and she couldn't help a pang that the words which came out of this one would not be her own but somebody else's—at least at first.

"What do you do here, Anna?" she asked, with a tug back to reality.

"I'm the bookkeeper." Anna sat down at her own desk and began dusting it off with a piece of cheesecloth. "I do other things, like sending stories out to be mimeographed, running the stamp machine, keeping track of stock, and relieving Patricia at the switchboard. I also type Mr. Kingston's letters. He writes them out himself. I don't know shorthand. I guess I do everything that no one else wants to do."

"Without which the office couldn't function," Edwina assured her.

"That's a nice thing to say, Edwina. It's all right if I call you Edwina, isn't it? You called me Anna. Besides, that's the way it is here. The men call us by our first names but we have to say Mr. Pritchard, and Mr. Odell, and Mr. Kingston."

"Why is that?" Edwina burst out. "That's absurd! Why should we say mister to a man who calls us by our first names?"

Anna sighed resignedly. "You'll get used to it. It's just an office custom."

Pat Evarts, pretty and fresh in a green linen suit, breezed in just in time to hear the last words.

"Hi, Anna. So you're teaching Edwina our office customs. They're some of them I'd be mighty happy without. Like our having only an hour for lunch. I've missed out on more luncheon dates because of that." She ran her comb through her absurdly snowy locks. "Don't let the men around here bother you, honey." This was addressed to Edwina. "Just remember they're only *men*. 'Bye now. I have to run. If Old Stick-in-the-mud doesn't find me at my desk, I'll get it for sure."

"Who is Old Stick-in-the-mud?" Edwina asked Anna, as Pat darted out.

Anna replied with a warning glance, and Edwina looked up to see Mr. Pritchard's secretary.

"Good morning, Miss Fiske. I see Anna has shown you where you are to work."

The frigid tone of Miss Dobbs' voice was a shock after the cordiality of the other two girls, but Edwina, bound she would get along with everybody in her new job, smiled at her warmly. "She's been very helpful. Have you anything for me to do until Mr. Odell gets here?"

"Not right now," Miss Dobbs said in a more kindly voice. "There's a conference at ten; I simply haven't time to explain anything. Anna, get her some press books. She can be looking through them. It will be your job to keep the clippings pasted up after this, Miss Fiske."

"That should be interesting." Edwina spoke with assumed cheerfulness, for her reaction was that she hadn't come to New York to play at cutting up paper like a kindergartner.

Anna disappeared into the stockroom to return with three large leather-bound volumes which she plopped down on Edwina's desk. "Here's the current tea book, the Golden Arrow and the air conditioners. Will that be all right, Dorothea?"

"Fine," Miss Dobbs said. "Study them carefully, Miss

34

Fiske. They will provide you with an excellent picture of the results of our company's campaigns." Her manner was that of a schoolteacher.

When she was gone, Anna said, "Dorothea works awfully hard really, and she's been here for years and years. They say she was real pretty when she was younger. But the only promotion she ever got was when Mr. Pritchard told her she could be office manager. It doesn't mean a thing because we all know our own jobs. But it keeps her happy to have someone to give orders to."

For the next half hour Edwina studied press books. The only other clipping book she had seen had been shown to her by a former actress, an old lady her father had sent her to interview for a feature article. That shabby book with its yellowed clippings had little resemblance to these handsome volumes, with all the items neatly pasted and labeled, each page covered with a sheet of transparent plastic.

"How elegant they are!" she commented to Anna.

Anna looked up from her ledgers. "Aren't they, though? Mr. Pritchard says that in accordance with the press books, so will a publicity firm be judged. We try to keep ours neat and well spaced. But when a story is syndicated we just paste up one or two representative clippings along with a typed list of all the other papers which used it. It isn't good to try to pad the books."

The two fattest ones were on tea and air conditioners, both of which showed the results of intensive work on the part of the Pritchard company. There were news stories, picture stories, feature stories, syndicated ones with a United Press or Associated Press dateline, others from

New York daily newspapers, financial stories, items from business and trade magazines, radio and TV interviews typed up or in mimeographed form.

The third book, the one on the Golden Arrow Bus Lines, had relatively few inserts, but among these were some Edwina could quickly see were worth hundreds of smaller items. They were a series of illustrated articles from *Fact,* one of the largest pictorial magazines in the country with a circulation in the millions. They were written by one of the editors who had been assigned to take a bus trip through the United States and who reported on the customs of different people in different parts of the country, the scenic wonders, the historical monuments. And the bus he traveled on was the new Airlift Golden Arrow. It mentioned this in each article, an odd thing for a magazine which usually steered clear of brand names in any form.

"It was a scoop to get this series in *Fact,*" Edwina could not help remarking to Anna.

"Wasn't it?" The bookkeeper's face lit up as though she were personally responsible. "Mr. Kingston arranged that when he first came here about six months ago . . . oh, we were just talking about you, Mr. Kingston." She broke off as that young man sauntered in.

"I thought my ears were burning." Pointedly ignoring Edwina, he went to the water cooler and poured himself a drink. "Beautiful morning, isn't it? What do you say, Anna, that you and I take off for a drive up to Connecticut?"

"Oh, stop your kidding," Anna said with an uncertain laugh. "He's always like this, Edwina. Mr. Kingston, have you met Edwina Fiske? She's the new girl here."

"Miss Fiske and I already have collided," he said. "I don't think she likes me, Anna. Will you tell her about my impeccable moral standards and stress that I only flunked out of three colleges?"

Before either of them could comment, Dorothea Dobbs returned, and with a disapproving look at the young man with "impeccable morals," went over to Edwina.

"Miss Fiske, Mr. Pritchard would like you to take the minutes at our conference this morning. I told him I wasn't sure you had the experience, but he insists. You had better take a couple of notebooks and several sharp pencils. You must be able to take down everything that is said."

"Oh, I forgot about that blasted meeting." Eric took his leave hastily.

"After the conference you can stop in my office and I will show you how we like the minutes typed," Dorothea continued. "They talk pretty fast sometimes. Do you think you'll have any trouble?"

"I don't see why I should," Edwina said, reassured that no matter how fast these gentlemen talked, they couldn't compete with old Judge Nordstrom once he started talking about his early days as a young lawyer.

The conference room was paneled in oak, with heavy yellow-and-brown drapes, a long polished table, and opaque glass ashtrays in front of each chair. Mr. Pritchard was at the head of the table and at his right was a man with a Vandyke beard and an austere intelligent face whom Edwina had not seen before. Eric was there, looking more dignified with his suit jacket on, and Mr. Odell slid in unobtrusively just as Mr. Pritchard rose to speak. Edwina, fortified with stenographic notebook and pencils, was farthest down the table.

"Ahem," Mr. Pritchard began by clearing his throat. "As some of you know, we are as of today publicity representatives of the Blue Star Book Club, one of the oldest and largest of such clubs in America. I don't need to tell you we are proud of this account. Blue Star books are the best in fiction and nonfiction. Those of you who read books can testify to that." He paused for an appreciative laugh.

"This is our problem, gentlemen," he continued, bringing the fist of his right hand down on the open palm of his left with a thud. "Five years ago the circulation of Blue Star hit its high peak of a million members. Since then they have been steadily losing circulation. This may be due to competition from other clubs, the History Book Club, the Classics Club, the Book Find and all the rest. Or it may simply be that members are deciding they are now smart enough to choose their own books." Again there was a pause and a murmur of laughter. "But whatever the reason"—Mr. Pritchard's voice rose—"we have to find it and see what we can do about it."

A pity he has only an audience of four, thought Edwina, as her pencil flew over the lined page. Mr. Odell had pulled out his pipe and lit it, as though he knew he was in for a long session. Eric Kingston was chain smoking. Only the stranger had neither cigarette nor pipe.

"I know our staff here is top-notch," Mr. Pritchard went on with a short laugh. "But for Blue Star I felt we needed a literature expert—an 'egghead,' so to speak." He didn't wait for a laugh on this but hurried on. "We have persuaded Dr. Vincent Rifkin here to handle Blue Star for us. He was formerly Professor of English at Midtown University, and for the last several years has been a free-lance book publicity agent. We consider ourselves fortunate he has consented to join our staff. Will you stand up, Dr. Rifkin?"

The man with the Vandyke beard stood up, said, "Thank you, Pritchard," and sat down again.

"Dr. Rifkin, I want to present you to the other members of our staff—Jeff Odell and Eric Kingston. And this is Miss Fiske," he added. "She will be doing your work as well as Jeff's."

That was news, and Edwina wasn't sure she liked it. She was familiar enough with office etiquette to know that if you worked for one man you were called a secretary, but that if you worked for more than one you were classified as a stenographer. On the other hand, book publicity sounded exciting, and she certainly wasn't yet in a position to say what she would and would not do.

"As I told you, Vince," Pritchard was saying with heavy informality, "we all co-operate with each other here. You must consider that all of us are here to help you. Jeff, for instance, knows every newspaperman in town and every bar they hang out in. Eric's father is publisher of *Fact*. When you have a story idea for them, he'll push it for you. He also gets around café society, which can be useful too."

The connection between Eric's father publishing *Fact* and Eric's success in placing the series of articles about travel via Golden Arrow Bus didn't register immediately with Edwina, intent on taking down every word of what was said.

After a few more remarks, mostly of a humorous nature, Mr. Pritchard yielded the floor—a bit reluctantly, it seemed to Edwina—to Dr. Rifkin.

The professor, or doctor as they called him, didn't bother to rise. His speech was pedantic with an occasional incongruous touch of modern slang. But it was obvious he knew what he was talking about. One of the mistakes of a great deal of book publicity, he said in effect, was that it was limited to sending out announcements and review copies to book reviewers. It was his theory that publicity should be directed to the great mass of people who rarely if ever read book reviews, and who had to be educated to the fact that books were not necessarily highbrow. His aim, he said, would be to get Blue Star, its selections and their authors in the news everywhere *but* in book review sections. That could usually be safely left to the publisher's publicity department. There would be a new author and a new book to promote each month, and each would present a different challenge and offer different opportunities for promotion. The September choice, for instance, was *The Way In* by Marjorie Appleton Gomez. Did any of them know about it?

No one did.

"Marjorie Gomez is a former high-school Latin teacher," Dr. Rifkin explained. "One day she took a sabbatical leave and went to Mexico to study art in a small university town. She stayed on to marry a Mexican and for the past ten years they have been running a small inn, catering especially to American students. The book is her own life, romantic but written with charm and humor. The lady is coming up to New York for 'pub' date. It's our big chance, since we'll have the author on the spot. I'd like to have your ideas for exploitation."

"If she's pretty, we might get the boys to run some good cheesecake shots of her," Eric contributed. His levity seemed in bad taste. Edwina half expected a rebuke from Mr. Pritchard. But though a small scowl appeared on his forehead, he made no comment.

"She is not a young woman," Dr. Rifkin said calmly. "I imagine anything at all vulgar or sensational would be offensive to her. No, we'll have to think of other angles."

The fact that he seemed to give serious consideration to Eric's proposal took the wind out of the younger man's sails. He looked uncomfortable and lit another cigarette.

They settled down to specific suggestions.

Jeff Odell named several women feature writers and TV and radio interviewers who might like to talk with this American woman who had changed a prosaic life for an adventurous one. Mr. Pritchard suggested having one of the "shelter" magazines send a reporter and photographer to Mexico to do a picture story of her inn, which combined American comforts with Latin picturesqueness. He had to explain to Dr. Rifkin that "shelter" was the term the publicity trade used for the big women's magazines such as *House and Garden, House Beautiful, The Ladies Home Journal* and *Good Housekeeping,* an explanation which Edwina appreciated since the expression was new to her too. They figured out different "slants" for publicity releases—one for food editors on how to adapt Mexican cuisine to the American home, another on the difference between the life of a typical Mexican housewife and an American one.

Finally the meeting was over. Edwina stopped in Dorothea's office, which opened on to Mr. Pritchard's larger one and also on to the hall.

"I hope you got it all," Dorothea said coldly. "The paper you will use for the minutes is on your desk. You will make four copies on onionskin, one for each of the men, and a fifth on Manila paper for our files." She handed her a loose-leaf notebook. "You will find the minutes of other office conferences in here. Follow their style for heading, spacing and capitalization." Her dismissal was a curt nod.

Dorothea's manner bothered Edwina for a few moments. Could it be that she resented her taking the minutes? She discounted the notion as soon as she got back to her own office.

"Was it fun?" Anna asked.

"Not too bad," Edwina told her. "Now the hard work comes."

She sorted the carbons and the paper Dorothea had left her, glanced at the previous minutes only long enough to grasp their form, and started typing. Routine as it was, she wanted this first sample of her work to be letter-perfect.

It was nearly one o'clock when she finished the last page and began sorting the pages. She was pleased with herself, for she had had no trouble reading her notes, and her manuscript was clear and clean with hardly any erasures.

"How's it coming, Edwina?"

She looked up to see Mr. Odell's ruddy face. "Oh fine, thank you. It's done."

"Good," he said. "May I take a look?"

With the confidence of a skilled craftsman, she handed him the first copy, the one that would go to Mr. Pritchard. As he scanned it an odd expression came over his face. "Mmmm . . . Did Dorothea show you any minutes from our other meetings?"

"Yes, she did," Edwina said, frowning in bewilderment. "I followed their format. Did I do something wrong?"

"Not exactly wrong." He skimmed through a few more pages. "But I think you'd better come into my office for a few minutes. Bring these." He indicated the copies of her minutes. "Also your notebook."

What was the matter? As she sat in his Victorian office, she studied his face, and it seemed to her that he was struggling not to laugh.

"Come on, tell me," she commanded him. "What is it?"

He took a long puff on his pipe. "You see, Edwina, taking minutes isn't quite the same thing as straight dictation. Sometimes some of us say things that look rather foolish on paper. In that case it's advisable not to be too literal."

"But . . ." She started to tell him that Dorothea had instructed her to take down every word but stopped herself. No matter what, she wasn't going to blame someone else.

"I think I'd better re-dictate some of this," he continued. "You will see what I mean. Ready?"

"Yes, Mr. Odell." Still puzzled, she nodded.

"We'll begin this way: 'The meeting opened with an announcement by Mr. Pritchard that the Blue Star Book Club had appointed Robert Pritchard and Associates as their publicity representatives. Dr. Vincent Rifkin had joined the staff to handle this account. The problem would be first to determine the causes for the decline in the Blue Star membership and then devise ways to increase the subscription list.' " He went on to give a summary of Mr. Pritchard's speech, leaving out his little jokes about "those of you who read books" and "an egghead, so to speak."

When he reached the point where Dr. Rifkin took over the meeting, he was much more detailed, and while he skipped Eric's crack about cheesecake, he was precise about listing in outline form all the more practical suggestions that had been made for publicizing the Mexican book.

"Do you get the idea, Edwina?" he asked when he had finished. "The purpose of the minutes is to remind us what our self-imposed tasks are in handling this account."

"I get the idea." Edwina looked at him disconsolately. The new minutes were dry and terse, but she was intelligent enough to know he was right. "I feel like a perfect idiot."

"Pooh," he said. "Someone should have explained the job to you more carefully, that's all. What you've done proves your steno is excellent. You have nothing to worry about. Now you'd better go get some lunch."

Instead she returned to her desk to type out the revised minutes. To her relief she was alone since Anna was at the switchboard. She didn't have to explain her blunder to anyone, and she somehow knew that Jeff Odell wouldn't say anything.

She was typing furiously when Anna joined her.

"You didn't go out to lunch, did you, Edwina? You should have. The minutes could have waited. Don't you want a sandwich sent up?"

Edwina shook her head. "Thank you, Anna, I'm not hungry."

"I'll make you a cup of tea, then. We can have tea here whenever we want it, did I tell you? There are some wafers, too. But you mustn't do this again."

By the time Dorothea stopped by after her lunch, the job was done and Edwina, strengthened with tea and wafers, felt more composed.

"Finished?" Dorothea asked. "Would you like me to check your work?"

"I'd be grateful," Edwina breathed.

She sat down at the vacant desk and read them through line by line. "These seem all right." Her voice expressed surprise. Then amazingly she smiled. "I think I must confess that I advised Mr. Pritchard not to hire you. I didn't feel you had sufficient business experience. I see now that I was wrong, and that Mr. Pritchard was right, as he usually is. I think you will be a real asset to the company, Edwina." She added as she headed for the door, "You must call me Dorothea from now on. We girls all call each other by our first names."

Chapter 4

Edwina spent her second day at the office typing envelopes addressed to city desks of daily newspapers in major
cities of the country. She didn't know what the envelopes
were for and nobody told her. The only interruption was
that Mr. Odell called her in to dictate a letter to the Army
Quartermaster Corps to check on an experiment under
way to offer tea to the Armed Forces at mealtimes as an
alternative to coffee. Halfway through the letter, he told
her to cross it off her book. A phone call to the Quartermaster would be a quicker way of learning how this project, initiated by the Pritchard office as part of their tea
publicity campaign, was turning out.

On Wednesday he called her in again to give her a form
letter, asking her to type up individual copies to some
fifty feature and society editors on newspapers and magazines. It was an invitation to a "tea-tasting contest" to be
held by the exclusive Epicure Club in one of the Waldorf
dining rooms the following week. Each guest, the letter
stated, would receive ten samples of tea, and the one who
could guess the names correctly would be the winner.

Thursday she had a different task. Harrison Dawes had sent over an assortment of photographs of members of his baseball team, the New York Wings, drinking tea with their trainer. Edwina pasted captions on the bottom of each print and typed out short news stories quoting the trainer as saying that he found tea to be the most suitable drink for his men in training.

"The Tea Conference Board will like this story," Mr. Odell remarked when she brought in the material for his final checking. "Do you know why?"

She shook her head.

"Because it shows good hundred-per-cent American athletes drinking tea," he said. "It illustrates that tea is not just a drink for ladies' sewing circles, and puts it on the sport pages instead of the society columns."

She was grateful to him for explaining this much to her and she told him so. He looked surprised.

But in the afternoon she went back to the dreary task of pasting up clippings.

On Friday, Dr. Rifkin, who had spent the last several days in the offices of the Blue Star Book Club gathering material, called her in to give her a copy of a weighty volume listing the names and circulation figures of weekly newspapers. Would she be good enough, he asked in his professorial manner, to go through the book and put a red check in front of all the weeklies which had a circulation of over a thousand?

By midafternoon she had reached the N's, and red checks danced before her eyes.

During these long four days she thought bitterly of how she had told Matt about the glamorous people she was sure to meet at her job. Aside from the office staff she saw

47

no one. She and Anna were left to themselves except when someone wanted one of them to do something. Their only regular visitor was young Eric Kingston. As though he had nothing else to do, he would hang around to kid Anna, accusing her, for instance, of going out with other men to make him suffer the torments of jealousy. To Edwina there was something cruel about the way he did this. It seemed obvious that he never suffered torments over anybody, much less this plain and eager young woman. His conversation with Edwina, on the other hand, was limited to a brief "Hi."

"Eric still doesn't think you like him," Anna said toward the end of the week.

"I'm not sure I do." Edwina shrugged. "He seems rather superficial."

"You don't understand him at all," Anna protested. "It's just his manner. You know, he has a wealthy family but he is so proud he won't take a penny from them. He insists on being independent."

"How did he get this job?" Edwina asked.

"I think Mr. Pritchard went to Yale with his father," Anna admitted.

Edwina didn't pursue the subject, returning to her red checks. She was still at it toward closing time when she had her first phone call.

"Miss Fiske?" The voice was deep and remotely familiar.

"Yes?"

"This is Harrison Dawes. You may not remember me. I met you last week in Jeff Odell's office."

"Of course I remember you, Mr. Dawes," she assured him warmly. "I'm sorry Mr. Odell has left for the day."

It didn't occur to her that it was anything but a business call.

"I asked for you, not Odell," he said clearly. "Would you have lunch with me on Monday?"

She couldn't believe her ears. "I don't understand."

"Would you be free to have lunch with me on Monday?" he repeated.

"Why, yes . . ." She was too surprised to sound enthusiastic.

"I'll meet you at the Château Rouge on 50th Street between Madison and Park at one o'clock. Is that all right?"

"That will be fine."

"Good. I'll see you then."

She hung up in a daze. Why on earth should a man like this Mr. Dawes, who gave every evidence of being affluent and important—in addition to being good-looking and who could certainly go out with any girl he chose—want to have lunch with her, whom he knew only as Mr. Odell's secretary? But as she sat motionless at her desk, her perplexity changed to anticipation. So far her lunches had consisted of sandwiches in the coffeeshop downstairs. To eat in a nice place in the company of a handsome escort would be a pleasant change. Because it was such an event in her life, she decided she must dress up to the occasion. She had her first week's pay in her bag; it seemed logical that one should splurge on one's first week's pay.

First there was her hair. She always at work wore it in the same fashion, parted in the middle and combed severely up in a roll on top of her head. She knew it was a good style for her, but it occurred to her that Margaret's hairdresser could make it look more glamorous. Monsieur Paul it was who tinted her aunt's hair its exotic blue tone, and Margaret said he was a genius at creating hair-do's "to suit one's personality." *Paul, hairdresser*. She found his address in the phone book, and before she could reconsider she telephoned, using her aunt's name as reference, and made an appointment for the next morning.

"You're daydreaming," Anna accused her when she came in. "I've never seen you like this before. You've been working too steadily. I've been worried about you."

"You don't need to worry about me," said Edwina, taking in a deep luxuriant breath.

Nevertheless she was a little worried herself when, after work, she walked down Madison Avenue looking at all the enticing frocks in the fashionable shop windows. She half wished she had waited and asked Margaret to go with her on her first New York shopping tour. But Margaret's taste in clothes was on the conservative side. She would probably have chosen something dull and drab. On her own Edwina decided on what seemed at the moment the most beautiful dress in the world, of yellow taffeta with small puffed sleeves, a low neck and a close-fitting skirt with a wide flounce at the bottom.

"It is stunning, simply stunning on you," the dour sales-lady assured her.

Farther on, where a shop advertised a hat sale, she purchased for a staggering price a few white daisies fastened together with a veil. "Exquisite," commented the beaming salesgirl. "Simply exquisite on you."

The next morning Monsieur Paul transformed her hair to a mass of golden ringlets. He had wanted to cut her hair, which was shoulder-length, and give her a perma-nent, but she wasn't prepared for such a radical step. Well, he said doubtfully, he would put lotion on madame's curls so they would perhaps stay curled for a few days. She kept a net on them the rest of the weekend and hardly dared sleep lest she disturb them.

On Monday, at five minutes past one, with hat, curls and dress, she reached the Château Rouge. Mr. Dawes was waiting for her at the entrance, every bit as attractive as she remembered him.

"I hardly recognized you," he said gravely as he guided her through the dimly lighted restaurant to a specially reserved table.

Even before the waiter seated her, Edwina, seeing the other women around her in their casual attire, realized that she was fearfully overdressed. The realization made her embarrassed; the embarrassment made her tongue-tied, a state so unusual for her that she was in misery.

"What will you have to drink?" her escort asked.

"Oh, nothing," she murmured.

"The chicken casserole with wild rice is a specialty of the house," he suggested. "It's very good. Would you like to try it?"

"Yes, thank you," she said.

The waiter took their order and departed.

"How do you like it at Pritchard?" he asked.

"Very much," she said. "It's a lovely place to work." The inanity of her own remark suffocated her.

He tried again, saying that publicity was an interesting profession. Had she read Charles Steinberg's new book, *The Mass Communicators?*

She hadn't. He told her about it. He went on to speak of some of the accounts his office was handling: a newly opened night club called The Gold Rush, which specialized in western and folk singers; a ballet school; a manufacturer of fine toilet soaps; a Swedish glass importer. "We like variety," he said. "It keeps us from getting bored."

She agreed this was an excellent plan.

As though convinced that publicity was the only subject that could interest her, he discussed some of the highspots in publicity history. There was the summer the Queen of England came to America and the publicity firm for the wool industries arranged for American wool interests to present a light wool dress to the Queen while Australian sheepmen presented a similar one to America's First Lady. Both were to be worn at their historic meeting, and thus set a precedent for light wool frocks for summer wear. And the time the National Cash Register Company's publicity agency arranged for a helicopter to take business editors to New Jersey to see the installation of a new electronic posting machine.

Real publicity was creative thinking and charting uncharted courses, Dawes said. That was the fun of it. The dean of all publicity gag men was Jim Moran, who began his career by selling an icebox to an Eskimo—for the icebox interests—and went on for other clients to hunt a needle in a haystack, take a bull into a china shop, and sell advertising space on the back of a whale. Still, this was only stunt publicity, for which Moran was remembered long after the names of his clients had been forgotten. The perfect publicity man stayed in the background as the power behind the throne. Didn't she agree?

She agreed again—and wished she hadn't. What a dud he must think her, without a mind of her own! Gallant and courteous as her host was, it seemed to her that this lunch would never be over. They were eating Strawberries

Romanoff when she noticed a woman at a nearby table waving to them. A moment later she quit her companion and came over to them.

"I didn't know you were eating here today, Harry," she exclaimed. "I don't mean to interrupt but I had to tell you I think it's going to work."

"Congratulations!" Dawes said. "Sit down a moment. Millicent, this is Edwina Fiske of the Robert Pritchard outfit. Edwina, this is Millicent Madden, my partner."

"I'm enchanted," Millicent said, as though she really meant it.

Edwina murmured something or other, noting that Miss Madden was petite, vivacious, with golden-brown hair cut in an informal Italian-style bob and a fashionable streak of white at the part, that she was dressed in a chic and simple black linen frock—that she was, in effect, just the way Edwina wished herself to be at that moment.

"How lucky you are to be working for Pritchard," Millicent was saying. "People say he's a real wizard. What are you doing, Harry, trying to pump her for some trade secrets?"

"I haven't got that far yet," he said, grinning.

"Let me know how you make out." She gave him a comradely pat. "I must rush back to my prospect. He's a shoe manufacturer, Miss Fiske, and he's putting out a new line of low-heeled comfortable shoes that are high style. Think what a blessing to working women who have to choose between high heels which torture them or sensible ones that make them look like frumps! I can hardly wait to get my fashion editors started on it. 'Bye, Harry. I'm so glad to have met you, Miss Fiske."

"Millicent is an enthusiast who believes a hundred per

53

cent in every one of our accounts," Harry commented when his partner had returned to her companion. "It's that which makes her a top publicity woman."

But of course he is in love with her, it stands to reason, Edwina concluded. The thought made her more self-conscious than ever. She couldn't imagine why he wasted his time on her.

"I wonder if you would have dinner with me sometime," he asked unexpectedly. "Say, next Friday night?"

And go through all this again, thought Edwina. Never! Aloud she said, "It's very kind of you, Mr. Dawes, but you see . . . my fiancé . . ."

"I didn't know," he said. "I'm so sorry. Shall we go?"

The long agony was finally over and she tore back to the office, for she was late. She still took time to stop in the washroom and give herself a cool critical survey in the mirror. It was worse than she imagined. Monsieur Paul's ringlets had not stood the three-day test and were coming loose. The expensive white daisy hat concoction had slipped to one side at a rakish angle. With her cheeks flushed more than usual, she reminded herself of a farmer's daughter after a hayride rather than a career woman. It didn't occur to her that her youth and good health had an appeal of their own, aside from her clothes. Deliberately she removed the hat, wet her comb, and pulled her hair back as tight as she could, fastening it with bobby pins. Never again, she resolved firmly, would she strive to be what she wasn't.

Chapter 5

The tea-tasting contest sponsored by the Epicure Club, for which Edwina had typed out invitations to the press, was held the following week. The guests included society people, explorers, writers, theatrical personalities, and celebrities in other categories all claiming to be gourmets, as well as a sprinkling of newspaper and magazine food experts.

In a private dining room hung with crystal chandeliers, they sat at tables with gleaming white tablecloths, sparkling silverware and tea service. At each place there were ten numbered packets of tea. A stream of tuxedoed waiters poured boiling water over each packet in turn, brought on fresh cups and whisked away the others, as the guests sipped, tasted, and wrote down their guesses on a printed card.

While the results were being tabulated, a reception was held where the guests intermingled. Finally the winner was announced. Surprisingly, the person who guessed all ten teas correctly, who knew the difference between Souchong and Oolong, Darjeeling and Jasmine, was not a professional gourmet, but a Wall Street broker. It made a nice little news story.

All of this Edwina learned not first hand but from the releases she typed up later and from the pictures taken by the photographers. Though all the men of the Pritchard staff attended, the girls, like good housewives, stayed behind to mind the office.

The tea-tasting party set the pattern for the days that followed. By the end of the month, Edwina felt she knew everything there was to know about the behind-the-scenes drudgery of the back office—and that she would never have a chance to get out of that back office.

She learned as much as she did about office routine not through Mr. Odell, who seemed to expect details to work themselves out automatically once he set a project rolling. Nor from Dr. Rifkin, who was new to the Pritchard setup. Nor even from Dorothea, who in her capacity as office manager should have given her instruction, for Dorothea, kept busy by her secretarial duties for Mr. Pritchard, had no time, and her office-manager title, as Anna had indicated, was just a way to let her enjoy some authority. She was no longer unfriendly, but Edwina saw little of her. Patricia Evarts, too, had become merely a pleasant face to whom she said good morning or good night. As for Mr. Pritchard, who had seemed so chummy when he hired her, he never came near the back office at all, and the only time she knew he was around was when she heard his voice down the hallway booming a greeting to some visitor.

It was Anna, the lowest paid and least impressive member of the staff, who with infinite patience guided her during those first difficult weeks.

When Mr. Odell dictated a publicity release and told Edwina to type out originals for the city desks of the New York dailies and have it mimeographed for the general list, it was Anna who translated his instructions. Original typed releases of important stories were sent to the seven New York dailies—as well as to the *Journal of Commerce* and the *Wall Street Journal*—because of the tendency of their busy news editors to throw mimeographed material into the wastebasket after a cursory glance. But costs would be prohibitive to send hand-typed releases to all the big city dailies, nor did they expect it. All mimeographing was done outside the office by the Fairfax Mimeographing Company; there were special forms for making out instructions to them which had to be initialed by the person who authorized the order. Anna would add such bits of information as that all releases, mimeographed or not, were mailed first class, because sealed envelopes received better attention than unsealed ones. That when publicity stories were delivered by messenger they should be timed to meet the paper's deadline. Or that if a story marked *Exclusive* was sent to a syndicate or a columnist, it must really be exclusive, else the publicity man would find himself in hot water.

Anna introduced Edwina to the intricacies of the filing system and helped her make up new files for Dr. Rifkin. She showed her the all-important media card file, subdivided under newspapers, magazines, radio and TV, with individual names of editors, columnists, feature writers, commentators and interviewers. "The first thing any publicity office does is build up its media list," she explained. "It's the connecting link between the publicity man and his outlets, and to be useful it must be kept up to date."

"My goodness, you know a lot about this place," Edwina commented with very real admiration.

"I should," Anna said gravely. "I've been here five years. I came right out of high school and at first all I did was filing and typing. Now you see I have more important work."

Her quiet pride in her small advancement to the position of bookkeeper was a lesson in humility—but did not augur well for Edwina's own future.

"If I could only do something to pay you back for all the help you've given me. . . ."

"There's one thing," Anna said hesitantly. "I do wish you'd be a little nicer to Mr. Kingston. It's so uncomfortable the way you treat him."

"I'll try," Edwina promised.

After that, when he hung around the back office—for no other reason she could see but to waste time—she'd say, "How are you today, Eric?" or something casual and friendly. She steadfastly refused to call this youth "Mr. Kingston" as Anna still did.

Her new attitude worked so well that once when Anna wasn't around he suggested they go stepping out some night—he'd like to show her a few night clubs. But at this she firmly drew the line. "Let's go on being friends—office friends," she said. "Okay?"

"Okay, if that's what you want," he agreed, and to her relief didn't press her further.

Harry Dawes had not telephoned her again and she tried to tell herself she didn't mind, which wasn't altogether true. She realized now that though she certainly hadn't been brilliant or scintillating at their lunch together, he wouldn't have asked her to dinner unless he had wanted her company, and she regretted having turned him down with such finality. Calling Matt her fiancé had perhaps been stretching the truth; he had never formally asked her to marry him. Moreover, ever since she had this job he had been treating her in a most cavalier fashion, not calling her for days and then, when he did call, expecting her to go out with him at half an hour's notice.

She tried to put romance and dates and dreams of a brilliant career out of her mind and to devote her energies to being a competent secretary.

It didn't take her long to discover that the two men she worked for, though both good publicity men in their own ways, were quite different, both in their characters and in the way they handled their jobs.

Jeff Odell, a former newspaperman, was a cheerful, gregarious person who had long since devised ways and means for doing what had to be done in the easiest, most pleasant way possible. He was never in the office before ten; he left a little after four to catch his commuter's train to Long Island. Nearly every day he had a long business lunch with some member of the press, and Edwina noticed that he invariably chose restaurants famous for their excellent cuisine.

When he called an editor about a news story, it was a long process in which information was exchanged about wives, children, fishing, boating, antiques, and how the tomato plants were growing. Friends and friends of friends were forever sending over someone who needed a job, and he was never too busy to call all over the city until he had arranged interviews for them.

With all this, he turned out a formidable amount of work. He knew instinctively what a good story was and where to place it. When he dictated a release, it was right the first time. Long years of making a deadline had taught him to work well under pressure.

Dr. Rifkin, in spite of his occasional slang and sometimes awkward use of the idioms of speech peculiar to Madison Avenue, remained essentially a scholar and a pedant. He dictated first drafts of news stories to Edwina, but these he edited and revised with the same loving care he might have given a literary thesis. He arrived early, stayed late, and took work home with him at night. Unlike Mr. Odell, he was not a family man and a commuter, but a widower who lived in an apartment in lower Manhattan.

In addition to his career as a professor and a publicity expert on books, he had written two volumes of poetry of his own. These had brought him small reward financially, but gave him a certain prestige. After an announcement appeared in the trade press and newspapers that he was handling Blue Star, members of the press frequently called him to ask for information not only about Blue Star authors but about any celebrated writer they wanted to contact, and as a general source of information about literary matters. When he talked to newspaper people he was brief and to the point, giving the impression he was trying to help them rather than to sell them something. They liked him, it seemed to Edwina, because he was so unlike the typical publicity man—that is, if there was a typical publicity man, which she was beginning to doubt.

Had she met either of the two men for whom she acted as secretary casually, perhaps in her father's newspaper office, undoubtedly she would quickly have become friends with them. She might have talked books with Dr. Rifkin or exchanged newspaper yarns with Mr. Odell. She told herself that couldn't be done in such an office relationship. Polite as they both were to her, she felt they must consider her, if not actually a servant, as belonging to a lower social order.

But they did like her work and that was already something.

On Friday at the end of her first month, Mr. Pritchard sent for her. A raise? He had heard how hard she had been trying?

"How are you getting along, Edwina?" He beamed at her, his manner as jovial as at her first interview. He didn't seem to realize that for a lapse of several weeks he hadn't spoken to her.

"Fine," she said.

"If you have any complaints you can always come to me, you know," he told her. "My door is always open to any member of the staff."

Her only complaint was her lowly position; she didn't think that would interest him.

"Thank you, sir."

"Do you know how to run the switchboard?" he demanded without further preliminaries.

She shook her head, wondering what prompted such a question.

"Ours is simple. At least so they tell me. I'd hate to be stuck with it myself." He grinned engagingly. "We want

61

you to take it over when Pat's at lunch and for her relief periods. Anna has too many other things to do. She or Pat will show you how to handle it. Clever as you are, you'll probably pick it up in half an hour. You don't mind, do you?"

What could she say? She made some noncommittal reply and got out of the office in a hurry before the company president could see how wretched he had made her. She was certainly making progress in her job—progress backward.

"They want you in the reception room because you are prettier than I am," Anna said later with a note of wistfulness. "I shall miss it. It was fun to go out and take telephone calls and see people come in and out."

We've both been made unhappy, thought Edwina, and neither of us has anything to say about the matter.

That night she had a date with Matt. For once he had the courtesy to call her up three days in advance, and he arrived on time. They went to Thornton's as usual. He seemed strangely uncomfortable.

"How's your job, Edwina?" he asked as he cut his steak.

"Wonderful," she lied. "It gets more interesting every day."

"Splendid," he said. "I knew all the time you'd make the grade."

"Thank you, Matt. How's *your* job?"

He didn't rise to the bait. "Edwina, there's something I've got to talk to you about." He breathed deep as though he were about to dive into an icy pool.

"Yes, Matt?"

"You know how I feel about you," he hurried on. "You know I think you're absolutely tops. You're way above me in everything."

"That's not so," she protested, half amused. "You've never seen me try to kick a football."

Instead of laughing he looked glum. "You're even wittier than I am. The truth is, Edwina, whenever I'm around you I feel like a clod."

"Since when, Matt?" she demanded, utterly astonished.

"I don't know exactly." He gave his steak a vicious slash. "Not at the beginning. At the beginning I felt like the big hero giving the campus orphan a build-up. I got a kick showing you around. Now you're way above me with your writers and your Waldorf tea parties and all that sort of thing."

"You've got me all wrong, Matt. I don't go to the Waldorf. I don't meet any writers. I just do the dirty work."

He didn't seem to hear her. "What I'm trying to say is you're going around with people where I just don't belong. Sooner or later you'll be ashamed of me. Let's don't kid ourselves."

She didn't ask him if there was another girl in the case. Somehow she knew with absolute certainty that there was.

"Would you like to call it quits, Matt?"

He moved restlessly in his chair, looking down at his plate. "I guess that's about it."

"But of course. You're perfectly free. You always were." The calmness of her own voice surprised her.

"You mean it?" The relief on his face was written large. "You're swell! You won't hold anything against me? We'll still be friends?"

"Naturally," she said, smiling very brightly. "Let's not even talk about it any more."

"Agreed," he sighed. "We'll go to the movies. There's a good Western down the street."

"You know, if you don't mind I think I'll let you go to the Western by yourself," she told him. "There's a lovely film at the Thalia, a French one I'd like to see. I know it would bore you silly."

Chapter 6

It was a beautiful morning, that Saturday, crisp and clear and sunny, with the tang of autumn already in the air. After a restless night, Edwina had risen at dawn, dressed herself quickly and quietly, and slipped out of the apartment without disturbing her aunt.

Following her "demotion" to part-time switchboard work and Matt's saying in so many words that they were through, she had to be alone. She had to think things out.

Her steps led her crosstown along the empty streets, west to Central Park, deserted at this hour except for an occasional rider on the bridal path. How peaceful it was! The trees were luxuriant in their late summer foliage; the sun had miraculously not succeeded in parching the soft grass carpet. Presently she found herself on a little bridge over one end of a lake where she watched the diamond sparkles on the tiny waves over which the ducks sailed like small and certain boats.

She knew she should be desperately unhappy, and yet somehow she wasn't. For the moment her own difficulties had become remote as a distant star, and the sun's rays seemed to flow through her, bringing a sense of well-being that defied logic.

A little farther along at an intersection of two paths an old woman stood feeding pigeons. She was a pitiful creature with straggly gray-streaked hair, a long uneven skirt, a man's unlaced shoe on one foot and a bedroom slipper on the other. But as she distributed the largess of the breadcrumbs in her crumbled paper bag, the pigeons swooping around her, alighting on her shoulders, her arms, her hair, her expression was beatific.

She saw Edwina and waved. "Mornin', my pretty little pigeon," she called. "Would you like a few crumbs?" She burst into cackling laughter that strangely had no malice in it.

"How they love you," Edwina called back. "Do you come here often, madam?"

"Every morning, dearie. These are my pets, my own darlin's."

Two of the pigeons, swooping over the same morsel, collided and started pecking at each other with ruffled feathers.

"There, there," the woman scolded, as she raised the sack and scattered the remaining crumbs. "Here's some for all of you. Ain't no need to be fightin' like that."

Edwina walked on down the path slowly. How could you measure success? Prestige or money or fame? The old woman had surely never tasted any of these and yet she seemed well content with her lot.

As she continued, she became aware that there was someone behind her. It bothered her. The park was hers that delightful morning. It belonged to her and the old woman with the pigeons. Anyone else was an intruder. She hastened her steps.

Then she heard a man's voice shout, "Let's go, Dodo," followed by the sharp responsive barking of a dog. A moment later a dachshund dashed by her, attached to a leash held by a tall youth in slacks and a gray sweatshirt. A boy and his dog—well, she guessed they had a right to be in the park too. They ran on a hundred yards or so and then stopped, both of them, as though they were waiting for her to catch up with them.

Of course they weren't, she reassured herself. They were just out of breath. She started to sail past them without a sideward glance.

"Nice morning, isn't it, Miss Fiske?"

There was something familiar in the deep timbre of the voice, and she stopped short, to meet the roguish smile and mischievous eyes of the youth in the sweatshirt.

She stared back in bewilderment until the features and the carriage convinced her that he was not a stranger. "Why . . . Mr. Dawes!"

"I didn't think you would recognize me."

"You look . . . different," she stammered. How very much different she could hardly say.

"You do too," he told her, his eyes taking in her cotton peasant skirt, her hair pulled back in a ponytail, her sneakers. "I still knew you, even in the midst of a half-mile dash. Oh . . . I want you to meet Dodo. Dodo, this is Miss Fiske."

The dog came over to her and, as she leaned over to pat him, waved his tail furiously and jumped up on her.

"He likes you. That's an honor. He usually snarls at

anyone we meet when we're out walking, though he's quite nice to anyone who comes to see us. His psychology is quite simple. Friends are those who visit us. Enemies include everyone out of doors. You are the exception." He frowned slightly as though this were something he couldn't figure out.

"I'm glad of that." Edwina knelt down on the grass and started scratching the dog under his throat. He responded by licking her hand and then trying to lick her face.

"That's enough, Dodo." His master pulled him back on the leash. "Do you mind if we walk along with you? A young woman shouldn't be alone in the park at this hour. It isn't safe."

She laughed. "I'm not afraid. You don't need to bother." Meeting him here out of all the millions of people in New York seemed a coincidence beyond comprehension.

"It's no bother," he said, falling into step with her. "A funny thing, your being here in the park, just where I always come."

"I still don't believe it's you." She gazed at him with increasing incredulity. "Why, you look ten years younger."

"I am," he said enigmatically. "You've only seen my business personality. I take it off on Saturday mornings —along with my glasses."

"That's right, you aren't wearing them. Shouldn't you be?"

He shook his head. "No. They're clear glass—to give me age and distinction. People wouldn't take me seriously, do you think, if they knew I was only twenty-four?"

"Why, you're only two years older than I am! I thought
. . ." She stopped.

"That I was old enough to be your father?" he finished
for her. "Well, I'm not. Do you mind?"

"Why should I mind? Only I still don't see why you
want to look older than you are. It reverses all the rules."

"I don't want to. I have to." He tugged at the leash
when Dodo tried to pull off to investigate a squirrel. "I'll
explain everything to you, if you like. Have you had
breakfast?"

She shook her head.

"On the terrace by the seals? Would you wait for me a
few minutes while I take Dodo home? The park attend-
ants have a funny notion that dogs and seals don't mix.
You might sit here." He indicated a bench half under the
shade of a large sycamore tree. "Don't go 'way."

"I won't," she promised, wondering at her own acquies-
cence. "Too bad we can't take Dodo." She leaned down to
pat him again, but the dachshund, straining at his leash,
ignored her now, and then the two of them dashed off,
vanishing around the bend of the path.

The moment they were gone, it seemed to her she had
imagined the whole fantastic episode. She was even
tempted to leave so she wouldn't be disappointed if he
didn't return. But a pleasant lethargy crept over her and
she didn't move.

A little old man in a shiny suit sat down on the far end
of her bench, after carefully wiping it off with his pocket
handkerchief, and began reading *The New York Times*.
Three boys of varying heights, carrying fishing poles, hurried along intent on big game. They separated to let pass
a Japanese with a camera over his shoulder and a tiny

black-haired child, dainty as an oriental doll, at his side. Behind him came an elderly couple, hand in hand, the man in a flowered shirt hanging loose over his trousers, the stoutish woman in a low-backed cotton dress incongruously wearing a vizor cap. They were followed by a couple of high-school girls in toreador pants, giggling and chattering like parakeets. The park was beginning to come alive.

Edwina hadn't begun to collect her thoughts or settle her problems when Harry Dawes was standing before her, slightly breathless and with beads of perspiration on his forehead.

"You're still here!" he exclaimed, as though she had accomplished something remarkable by not vanishing. "We'll eat now. I'm starved."

As they walked off he nodded his head in the direction of the little old man on the bench, who hadn't looked up from his paper. "I told you Central Park wasn't a safe place for young women alone. You see what happens when my back is turned."

Edwina broke out laughing. Her companion turned to her with a look of mild astonishment, and then he laughed with her. In that delightfully good moment Edwina found time to reflect that it was a long time since she and Matt had laughed together.

Harry Dawes seated her beneath a parasol on the terrace of the zoo cafeteria, went off to return with a tray bearing tall glasses of orange juice, toasted English muffins, scrambled eggs and coffee. Edwina helped him clear the tray and set their places.

"I think I like this better than the Château Rouge," she said.

"I do too," he agreed. "I like this fine. Now tell me who you are and what you do."

"You know what I do."

"I know nothing. Except that from nine to five on weekdays you report to work for Robert Pritchard and Associates. But what do you really do—when you're not pretending to be a secretary?"

It was a tempting opening to talk about herself, but Edwina wasn't prepared for it yet.

"First I want to know how you manage to be a successful publicity man at the age of twenty-four."

"I'll give it to you straight," he said with a mock conspiratorial air. "In the first place Madden and Dawes is not yet really successful. We have some nice accounts, but they are comparatively small ones and we barely meet expenses, which are high. But I will be successful because I have to be." He made the latter statement as a fact, without bragging.

"How did you get started?" she pressed him.

"I made up my mind what I wanted to do while I was in college," he said. "It was a process of elimination. I couldn't be a doctor or lawyer or engineer—there was no money for additional schooling. I didn't want to be a teacher, knew I couldn't take buying or selling something in the commercial field, lacked the predilection for solitude a writer must have, and wasn't cut out to be a newspaperman. All that was left was publicity."

"As simple as that!" she exclaimed. "What happened next? One can't overnight make oneself into a publicity agent—or can one?"

"No," he said. "It has to be learned like any other profession. I had to earn while I learned. When I got out of

71

Harvard, I made the rounds of the big publicity offices until I found one that needed an office boy—a place called Sperling and Smith that does theatrical publicity. You've heard of it?"

"I have." Edwina almost blushed to remember that was one of the places where she had offered her own services as a publicity writer—and been turned down cold.

"I opened mail, ran the mimeograph machine, folded publicity releases, sealed them in envelopes, put postage stamps on them and lugged them to the post office, pasted up clippings and was allowed to do filing—a wonderful way to find out what's going on. I asked questions of everyone who had the patience and inclination to answer them, and it was surprising how many people did, including city-desk editors, photographers, and lady columnists, to all of whom I made deliveries from time to time. At night I did my homework. By the end of six months I felt myself fully qualified to handle a publicity account. If I'd been in your position, as a secretary, I could probably have done it in three."

"You're boasting," she said, sipping her coffee.

"No, I'm not. Honestly. It all depends on the way you apply yourself. A man can live in a foreign country twenty years and not know the language, or he can master it perfectly in less than a year, if he decides that's what he wants to do. It's the same way with publicity. That is, if you have an aptitude for it—as I think you would if you tried."

She skipped over that. "What did you do after your six months with Sperling and Smith?"

"I got a job doing publicity," he said, as though that

was the easiest thing in the world. "I'd made one friend among the executives at Sperling who had as much confidence in me as I had in myself and who gave me a reference. I borrowed money to buy some ridiculously expensive clothes—and a pair of glasses. Having added the necessary ten years, I became publicity man for the Association to Aid Fatherless Children."

This sort of publicity was called fund-raising purely, he continued, over a second cup of coffee, but the techniques were pretty much the same as in any other publicity. The Association aided women who had lost their husbands and who were trying to keep their children with them. Money was raised to buy food and clothing and such necessities for the half-orphans. The Association also enlisted "foster parents" who would send packages regularly to the families.

"That's enough shop talk," he announced. "Let's go look at the monkeys."

The monkeys amused them for a good half hour, particularly a chimpanzee who was concentrating on making a finger painting out of lettuce leaves and cottage cheese on the floor of his cage. Then they visited the lion, the tiger, the jaguar, the hippopotami and the polar bears, with all of whom Harry seemed on the most intimate terms.

"After too many business conferences, I always come here and talk with my friends. It restores my sanity," he explained.

Afterwards they strolled north again, this time on the east side of the park. They had reached the small artificial lake in the Seventies and were eating buttered popcorn bought from a vendor and watching small boys sail toy boats with red and blue sails when Edwina brought up publicity again.

"How long did you work for the fatherless children? How did you happen to leave?"

"My friend at Sperling," he said, "the one who gave me the reference, was Millicent Madden. She decided to go out on her own and asked me to come in with her. That was all there was to it."

Was it all? Though she now realized he was younger than Millicent, the years wouldn't matter too much if they really cared for each other. Besides, they had so much in common. Though she and Harry had been talking like old friends, she suddenly felt like a stranger.

"Do you like going to the Metropolitan Museum?" he asked.

"I've never been. I always intended to but never found time, somehow."

"We'll do a small corner of it," he suggested. "Come on. We're almost there."

The long columned building impressed her, giving her the feeling of being transported to Italy or France or Greece. Once inside, he led her along the corridors to meet his special "friends," which he had here as in the zoo—a thirteenth-century saint carved in wood and wearing an expression of untouchable serenity, a Chinese holy man in porcelain sitting crosslegged and looking down on them with a mixture of wisdom and whimsy, a plaster bust of Voltaire by Houdon, Rembrandt's *Old Woman Paring Her Fingernails*.

"I always feel if I didn't pay my respects to them first,

74

their feelings would be hurt," he told her with the utmost gravity.

Their respects paid to these favorites, they wandered at random through the Egyptian section, the Early American Wing, the galleries of armor and ancient weapons. Lunchtime went by unnoticed and their absorption was so complete that it was hours before Edwina realized how tired she was.

"I'm sorry, I cannot walk a step further," she confessed as they paused to admire a giant Etruscan warrior in terra cotta.

He looked down at her with amusement. "I was waiting for you to say it. Few girls could have lasted so long. We must have done ten miles. The rest will wait. We'll have tea. They have a cafeteria too, though it's real fancy."

Very fancy indeed, it seemed to Edwina, as he led her to the rear of the South Wing into the former Pompeian Court room, with its striking black walls and white grillwork, and the pool and fountain in the center with the Muses—the concept of a Swedish sculptor—rising out of the water. Harry seated her at a small table by the pool and again did the honors, returning with a tray piled full with cakes, sandwiches, salads, and tall glasses of iced tea.

When she protested at the quantity, he explained: "I like it here but I'm against it in theory because there's a seventy-five-cent cover charge—too much for a lot of people. I wanted us to get our money's worth."

"We get our money's worth just being here," Edwina said happily.

As they were eating, he fell silent. She watched him

thoughtfully. No, he wasn't really handsome—not as she had thought at first. There was nothing sleek and smooth about his features. His hair, unruly now, had a widow's peak, on either side of which the hairline receded sharply. His eyebrows arched sharply at the center, giving him an impish look concealed usually by his glasses. But now his expression was absent-minded.

"Is something bothering you?" she asked.

He scratched his head . . . "Oh . . . oh, I guess so. I was thinking of Mr. Rierdon. He's my client who makes soap."

"What about him?"

He looked sheepish. "He has no right to come haunt me here. Let's forget about him."

"Come on, out with it," she urged. "What's wrong with him?"

"There's nothing wrong with him," he told her, munching a sandwich. "He's one businessman I admire. That's the trouble." In response to her inquiring look, he shrugged. "Well, you asked for it."

Mr. Rierdon, he confided, was a patron and one of the most active members of the Association to Aid Fatherless Children, which was how Harry had met him. His firm was an old one handed down from father to son, which specialized in quality soaps, and the nice thing about him was that his philanthropies were not limited to outside charity but extended to his own employees. He had remodeled his factory, over in the warehouse district next to the Hudson, along modern lines. It was light, airy, clean, with a large room in the basement for recreation purposes. The workers received the highest pay in the industry, were provided with free hospitalization, a nurse on the premises and a doctor part-time. They were given generous bonuses and participated in a profit-sharing plan.

"It sounds wonderful," Edwina said.

Harry nodded. "It's the nearest to it of any place I know. The thing is he doesn't give a hoot whether his soap is mentioned in the papers or not; he has his steady customers. He's no more interested in personal publicity. But he's proud as anything of his factory. His thought is that if the newspapers would print something about it, other companies would see what he has done, still making a good profit, and it would serve as an example everywhere. Maybe that's so and maybe it isn't, but in our business the client is always right. If the factory were in a small town we could at least get some local publicity. But in New York, no one cares, or so it seems."

He paused to drink his tea.

"There ought to be something that would make reporters come and look it over. A big party for the employees, perhaps," she said.

"Still not a news story." He shook his head. "Unless . . ." He paused. "Unless it could be a party for the benefit of the Fatherless Children . . . no, that's not enough."

"The employees might give a tea party for the Fatherless Children. Then Mr. Odell could help you," Edwina suggested facetiously.

He didn't laugh. "That's an idea . . . if we could get enough celebrities there."

"Too bad you don't have a famous movie star at your beck and call," she said jokingly as she selected a cream puff from a plate of cakes.

He stared at her. "You know what? There is one."

"What do you mean?"

"Arlene Dare." He named one of Hollywood's more popular young actresses. "Rierdon told me she was once a wrapper in his factory. She had a different name then, Irish, I think. I wanted to make something of it at the time, but Rierdon was against it. But perhaps if his favorite charity were involved he would react differently. It's worth thinking about." He began to eat his food as though he enjoyed it.

"You feel better now?"

"Much better," he said. "Now you do the talking. What does your fiancé do?"

What could she tell him? That only the night before her alleged fiancé had with many a compliment freed her of any claim on him? She was much too proud. Instead she explained, as well as she could, about the Blanchard Service, expecting him to look properly bored. He wasn't.

"It sounds like a natural for a publicity campaign. You ought to get him and Pritchard together. It would be a big feather in your cap to get an account like that."

"You're talking shop again," she reminded him.

"You caught me that time." He grimaced, then looked at his watch. "Do you know it's nearly five o'clock? If we don't get out of here, we'll be put out."

When they were outside on the museum steps, he said, "I have to rush off now. I have my children to feed." He didn't explain this baffling statement. "Can I leave you off somewhere?"

Edwina shook her head, inexplicably saddened. "I'll take a crosstown bus. I had an awfully nice time. Thank you so much."

He didn't seem to notice her sudden stiffness. "There's a cab now," he said. "So long."

She watched him as he tore down the steps two at a time. Even in his outrageously collegiate clothes there was an air of mastery about him that caused the taxi driver to pull up quickly at his signal. She realized with a pang that even after all his confidences, she still knew very little about him and the sort of life he lived.

Chapter 7

"Could you let me have five dollars until the end of the week?"

Edwina was alone in the office pasting up clippings when Eric wandered in and made this request for a loan. It was not the first time. At first he had paid her back on schedule but one Friday he had given her only three of the five he owed her and the week before he hadn't paid her back at all. Considering the wealthy family she had heard so much about, it was very puzzling.

"Broke so soon after payday?" she asked. "What do you do—bet on horses?"

"Don't give me a hard time, beautiful." He leaned over and put his arm across her shoulders with an air of familiarity.

The gesture as much as his request for money irritated her. "I don't have five dollars and if I did I wouldn't give it to you," she said crossly, shrugging him off. "Run along now and let me get some work done."

"Be a sport," he persisted, although he removed his arm.

"Get out," she commanded him, more good-humoredly.

"You're missing a great opportunity by not investing in my future."

"I'll take that risk."

He made a face at her and turned and went back into the stockroom where Anna was.

He came back a moment later, ostentatiously carrying some newly sharpened pencils—the pencil sharpener was in the stockroom—and headed for his own office without speaking. He was closely followed by Anna, who went to her desk, took out her handbag from the bottom drawer where she kept it, and left the room.

Briefly a suspicion flashed through Edwina's mind, but she didn't have time to dwell on it. She had too much to do. Since the day with Harry in Central Park, she had stopped pitying herself because she was classified as a secretary or a stenographer or an alternate receptionist and switchboard operator. Now she could take a more objective view of her situation. The fact that Harry worked as an office boy for a period hadn't made him an office boy forever. The same could be true of her.

Like Harry, she was learning to ask questions of "anyone who had the time and inclination to answer them." Jeff Odell was proving her best bet. He had the instincts of a born teacher, as she should have seen the first time she met him. He was only too willing to explain to her, if she asked him, why he would send out a certain story to a certain publication. In fact, he seemed pleased she was interested. With a little prodding she could also start him talking about his past newspaper and publicity experiences. Gradually a quiet camaraderie was developing between her and this old-timer.

While Dr. Rifkin wasn't much on reminiscing, she found out he liked having her as an audience to talk out his various ideas for Blue Star publicity. Occasionally she could even make useful suggestions. For instance, he was working up an idea for a book column to be sent in mimeographed form to weekly newspapers, to mention not only Blue Star books and authors but books of other publishers. He had been laying the groundwork for this project when he had asked her to check all the weekly newspapers with circulation of over a thousand. Now he was planning a letter to go to these editors with a return postcard, asking if they could use such a service.

"Have you considered offering the column as a newspaper mat?" Edwina proposed tentatively. "That way the editor could put it right on the press without the expense of setting type. Some of the papers might be more willing to use it in that form." She was speaking from her experiences in her father's office.

"That is not a bad idea," he said. "I'll buy it." (More of his current slang.) "Can you get me the costs?"

A little searching through the Red Book directory and a few telephone calls, and she had found a mat service that would make mats up for them in quantities at a reasonable fee. With the approval of the president of Blue Star, who had to foot the bills, their letter of inquiry to weekly newspaper editors asked whether they would prefer the book-column service in mimeographed or mat form. About half of those who replied said they might use the service regularly if mats were provided.

Publicizing tea presented a different challenge, more in the field of public relations than publicity, since the campaign was concerned with changing the public's attitude toward tea. Ever since the Boston Tea Party, tea drinking had been in bad repute in America, Mr. Odell pointed out. He told her that the first step they had taken on getting this account was to make a "motivation research study" to find out why people change from any product to which they are accustomed. It turned out it was usually because they were not satisfied with the old product, not because they wanted to try something new. Accordingly they had geared the tea campaign to convince people that tea had qualities no other drink provided—that it was both stimulating and relaxing, nonfattening and yet sustaining. As in any other form of publicity it took repetition and patience to get such ideas across. Molding public opinion is not accomplished overnight.

As her self-imposed homework these days, Edwina was devoting herself to a careful study of newspapers and magazines, always with a view to learning the type of stories that various editors and feature writers liked and could use. When she had a chance she listened to interview programs on the portable radio in her room. She did the same with television programs whenever Margaret was out. She couldn't do this when her aunt was home, for Margaret detested TV on principle. She turned it on only for an opera or a Shakespeare play or some cultural or educational program. Otherwise it was kept concealed behind a Chinese screen.

To this intensive homework Edwina now added reading a large tome on the history of tea, which she borrowed from a branch of the New York Public Library. The book, much of which was concerned with statistics about tea consumption and tea production, was brightened by some interesting anecdotes. It occurred to her that some of these might be used as fillers for the food-page editor or items for columnists.

The night before she had the run-in with Eric, she had re-written several of them: one about the origin of iced tea, which happened at the St. Louis World's Fair; another about the first tea bags, also an American contribution to the tea industry; an item about tea drinking among the Russian Cossacks (whom nobody could term sissy!); one about William Hazlitt, the English essayist, who had the reputation for drinking the strongest tea in the world —he always filled his teapot half full of tea leaves before he added boiling water, and drank some forty cups a day of this thick brew.

They were typed up neatly on her desk, and when Mr. Odell rang for her shortly after Anna's disappearance with her handbag, she took them along, together with her pencils and notebook.

There were two paper cartons on his desk.

"Good morning, Edwina," he said. "Here's your coffee. You can do the honors."

Mr. Odell always had coffee sent up the moment he arrived in the office, a curious habit for a man handling a tea account. The last week or so he had been ordering some for his secretary too. She welcomed the short interlude because it was a fine time to discuss publicity in general.

"I suppose you have a lot of work lined up for me today?" he asked cheerfully, as she removed the carton tops and served him his coffee with a paper napkin, a wooden spoon and two lumps of sugar.

He was joking, but it gave her the opening she needed.

"As a matter of fact, I have. I've been spending my

spare time on just that problem." A month before, pre-Central Park as she put it in her own mind, she wouldn't have dared speak to him in this fashion.

"Out with it," he said. "What have you been up to?"

She sat down and handed him her little stories. "Please read these and see if they would fit in anywhere."

He glanced through them as she drank her coffee and tried to convince herself it didn't matter what he thought.

"Mmm . . ." he said. "What do you want to do with them?"

"I'm not sure. I thought maybe as fillers on a food page."

"Send them over to Adele Fromm of Riley Syndicate," he suggested. "She might be able to work them in." He added, "Suppose you do another one about the fact that Americans consume 30 billion cups of tea a year."

With no other comment, he turned to his own work, dictation of a story about the accomplishments of the Tea Conference Board for a business magazine.

She went back to her desk elated. Though Mr. Odell hadn't praised her writing, the fact that he had told her to send the items out—and even suggested an additional one—was proof enough that he liked her idea. She typed his name on the note she wrote to Adele Fromm, the food editor for Riley Syndicate, and took it into him to sign along with his own dictation.

"You could have signed this one yourself," he said.

"I think Mr. Pritchard would like it better this way."

He shrugged as he pulled his fountain pen from the old-fashioned bronze holder. "Maybe you have a point there." He added, as she started to leave, "I'll tell you

85

something, Edwina. Initiative is a good thing, even here. It doesn't always pay off immediately, but don't let that bother you."

At twelve o'clock, as usual, she took Patricia's place at the reception desk. Now that she had decided it wasn't beneath her dignity, she liked this assignment. Things were quiet at the noon hour, and she could continue her homework by reading the trade magazines to which the office subscribed. Oddly enough, reading magazines was permissible at the desk though it was not considered proper to read either books or newspapers. Just what the difference was, no one tried to explain.

Anna could take her lunch hour when she wished now, and came out about twelve-thirty.

"I have to go to my bank, Edwina," she said in a low whisper. "I may be a little late. Please explain if anyone asks for me."

She still looked dispirited and unhappy. Eric's request that morning followed by Anna's exodus, and now the bank—it began to add up.

"Anna, have you been loaning money to Eric?" Edwina demanded bluntly.

Anna stared at her bleakly. "Don't say anything, Edwina, please don't," she half-sobbed, and without another word dashed out of the office.

In the afternoon Edwina took dictation from Dr. Rifkin. Señora Gomez, the author of the book about her marriage to a Mexican and her life in Mexico, which had been discussed at Edwina's first office conference, was now in New York for her book's publication. Dr. Rifkin had been piling up interviews for her, in between preparing feature stories.

Today he was intent on another matter, composing a letter to the Blue Star Book Club members explaining a plan whereby each member who brought in a new subscriber would receive a bonus gift of a beautifully illustrated and handsomely bound edition of Cervantes' *Don Quixote*. This sort of thing was properly termed promotion, but Dr. Rifkin was good at writing convincing sales letters, and it had become part of his regular job.

His phone rang just as he finished dictating, and Edwina heard him talking to Mr. Lindquist, President of Blue Star.

"Type this letter I just dictated right away, if you will," he said when he hung up. "Lindquist insists I bring it over personally at four o'clock. He is always in an insane hurry for such matters."

"Yes, Dr. Rifkin."

"Oh, good Lord," he said suddenly, clasping his hand to his head, "I forgot. I have a rendezvous with the Señora and Max Deerfield at four-thirty at the Knowlton Towers Little Bar." He glanced at Edwina with a sheepish smile. "It is the absent-minded professor in me, you will say. Maybe Jeff will take over." He picked up his phone, but Patricia told him that Mr. Odell hadn't been feeling well and had already left.

"I'll bet my bottom dollar"—another of his favorite expressions—"I'll bet my bottom dollar he's taken off fishing. There is still young Eric."

But when Patricia connected him with Eric, Eric told him unfortunately he had an appointment with the managing editor of *Business News* at the same hour.

"Pritchard's out too, isn't he?" he asked Edwina.

Yes, Edwina confirmed that Mr. Pritchard was taking a long weekend in Connecticut.

He sighed. "What to do? I cannot let her go alone for she is shy as a woodcock. Mr. Deerfield will terrify her."

"I'll go with her if you like," Edwina volunteered.

"You will?" The notion seemed to bother him for a moment and then he relaxed. "After all, why not? Yes, on thinking it over, I like it. I am sure you could do an excellent job. You know Mr. Deerfield?"

Edwina didn't. He was only a name on a card file to her.

"That doesn't matter. You let him do the talking and let him ask the questions. Your role will be to give the Señora your moral support. She'll be here at a quarter after four, and you will take her to the Knowlton in a taxi. I suppose you know you will have to pay for the drinks. Do you have any money, may I ask?"

"Not much," Edwina admitted.

He reached into his wallet. "Here's my American Express Credit Card. All you'll have to do will be to write a tip onto the check and sign it in my name. It will be less embarrassing for Mr. Deerfield than if you paid cash. Nearly all publicity people use these gadgets nowadays. And here's a couple of dollars extra for taxis. Tomorrow you will make out an expense slip for me to sign. Thank you, Miss Fiske." Unlike the other men in the office he didn't use her first name. "I'm very grateful to you."

She refrained with difficulty from saying she felt she was the one to be grateful to him. Already she had to admit she had certain advantages as a secretary which had been lacking to Harry during his office-boy period.

Chapter 8

Edwina left word with Patricia to let her know when the lady author arrived, but Dorothea, who happened to be in the reception room, was the one who came in to inform her.

"Where is Dr. Rifkin?" she demanded. "He knew he had an appointment with Señora Gomez. She's waiting for him. He shouldn't do things like that."

Edwina explained the situation.

"No one consulted me about it." Dorothea was obviously indignant. "Where is Odell?"

"He wasn't feeling well; he left early," Edwina told her.

"It seems to me he's leaving early a little too much lately," Dorothea said sharply.

It wasn't a nice thing to say. Edwina bit her lip to repress a sharp retort.

"I'm sorry," Dorothea apologized, recognizing Edwina's silent reproof. "It's just that I feel so responsible for everything when Mr. Pritchard is away. Next time anything like this happens, come in and tell me about it, Edwina." She stalked out, leaving Edwina in peace to put on her jacket and arrange her hair.

Anna looked up from her ledger. "I think she's a little jealous that Dr. Rifkin asked you to go and not her."

"I asked myself," Edwina told her. "It was all my idea. Anna, I do so want to make something of this job."

"You're very clever," Anna said. "You will succeed, I know you will."

"Thank you, Anna. Please wish me luck on my first interview."

"Oh, I do," Anna assured her earnestly.

Señora Gomez was a faded, gentle little woman with big brown eyes, blond hair going gray, and a serene smile; she wore a badly tailored tweed suit. She seemed not in the least upset that Dr. Rifkin had left her to the tender mercies of his secretary.

"I'm glad you're going," she said in a loud stage whisper as they rode down in the elevator. "I feel more comfortable with a woman along." She gave a little laugh. "I guess I've become a real Mexican housewife who feels it sinful to walk down the street with any man who is not her husband. If I hadn't had a sister in New York I don't think I would have found the courage to come at all."

In the course of the taxi ride to lower Park Avenue, Edwina discovered that Señora Gomez was just as her book indicated, simple and childlike and still full of wonder that a handsome dashing man like Señor Gomez could have wanted to marry her.

The Knowlton Towers Little Bar was a meeting place for writers, publishers, theatrical people, and the more prosperous members of the "communications" world. In her black wool frock which Margaret had selected for her, with very short sleeves and high neck, Edwina this time felt as smartly dressed as anybody.

Max Deerfield was not there when they arrived. Edwina, with a sense of protectiveness for her companion, asked the waiter to find them a table and notify the columnist where they were when he came.

"How well you do this sort of thing, dear," Señora Gomez said as they took their seats. "It's a real art handling oneself in places like this, isn't it?"

Edwina had to laugh. "I'll tell you the truth," she confided. "I've never been in a New York bar before in my life except once or twice with my boy friend." She should, more correctly, have said ex-boy friend, but that would have entailed explanations that were not in order.

Ten minutes late on the dot, Max Deerfield strode toward them, a big imposing man with bushy iron-gray hair. He looked older than the picture which topped his column. The column dealt theoretically with what was going on in New York, but he managed to weave in a great deal of extraneous information. It ran daily in the New York *Globe* and was widely syndicated. Few columnists had as extensive an audience as he did, a fact which the arrogance of his movements indicated he was aware of.

He looked at them both as though the waiter had misdirected him, and started to walk past. Edwina had to call him.

"Mr. Deerfield!"

"Yes?" He arched his eyebrows into an inquiring frown.

"Dr. Rifkin sent you his apologies, he could not be here. I'm his assistant, Edwina Fiske. This is Señora Gomez."

The word "assistant" came out as if by accident.

"Oh?" He paused, seeming to weigh the truth of her statement, and then smiled. "This is an unexpected pleasure. I'm delighted to meet you, Señora Gomez. Miss Fiske." He sat down.

"I was in Mexico a year or so ago," he began without preliminaries, and went on to recount his difficulties with custom officials and his problem in finding a good hotel, since the one where he customarily stayed was closed due to earthquake damage.

His monologue was interrupted by the waiter, who, seeming to size up the situation, glanced at Edwina for the order.

"What would you like to drink, Mr. Deerfield?" she broke in.

"Oh, Scotch and soda, I guess." His tone was indifferent, though he added the brand he preferred.

"And you, Señora?"

Señora Gomez looked embarrassed. "Why, I don't really know . . ." Her voice trailed off.

"Why don't you have a dry sherry?" Edwina proposed —dry sherry being the one drink her aunt allowed herself. When Señora Gomez said that would be fine, she ordered a lemonade for herself.

"I see I don't have any heavy drinkers here," Deerfield said with misdirected humor, and proceeded to expand on the subject of Mexican politics, the influence of American importations on Mexican economics, and other subjects of like nature about which Edwina suspected Señora Gomez knew little or nothing. Nor did he seem to expect her to express an opinion for he answered all his own questions without even waiting for her comments.

What a dreadful boor, thought Edwina, disillusioned. It seemed to her that a columnist of all people should show more interest in what other people thought and not lose himself in the sound of his own voice. Her thoughts strayed and she found herself looking around the room to see if there was anyone there she should know. She thought she recognized Anna Maganini, but on closer observation decided it was merely somebody that looked like her. But she was pretty certain a man at another table was Erich Maria Remarque, and that gave her a thrill for *All Quiet on the Western Front* was one of the few war stories she really liked. Then at a table quite close to them she saw one person whom she knew she knew—Eric Kingston. He was in the company of a plump blond girl in décolleté cocktail dress, and heavily made-up, who she was quite certain was not the managing editor of *Business News*. His eyes met hers at the same moment, and quite deliberately, without a sign of recognition, he moved his chair so that his back was to her.

Max Deerfield was still talking, having switched to trips to other Latin American countries, and the trials and tribulations he had endured on each one. Señora Gomez was listening with a rapt air, behind which Edwina sensed an inner amusement. Edwina was strongly tempted to interrupt and remind the columnist that he was supposed to be doing the interviewing. She remembered in time Dr. Rifkin's admonition to let him do the talking and ask the questions, and restrained herself.

He was on his third Scotch and soda when he finally got around to his first question. "Is it true you were a Latin teacher before you went to Mexico, Señora?"

He knows very well it is true, Edwina thought crossly. That bit of information was included in the background notes they had sent over to Deerfield before the interview.

When the Señora further confirmed it, he launched into a tirade against his own childhood Latin teacher, and in fact against the whole system of teaching Latin in high school. Oddly enough this broke the ice. The author, all timidity forgotten, began ardently defending her profession, and then somehow she was talking to him as an old friend, explaining just how she happened to take her sabbatical in Mexico, her secret interest in art, what her life was like there, even showing him pictures of the little boy that was the product of her late marriage.

There was method in his manner of approach after all, Edwina conceded with renewed respect for the columnist.

It was after six when he glanced at his watch. "Time is something I'm always forgetting and which is always catching up with me," he announced genially. "I was supposed to be at Twenty-One to meet the designer of that new transatlantic steamship half an hour ago."

Edwina signaled the waiter. "Check please."

It proved not too difficult to pay a man's bill after all. Mr. Deerfield was ostensibly talking intently to the Señora, unaware of what was going on while Edwina gave the waiter Dr. Rifkin's credit card and wrote on the slip the additional sum for a tip.

The Little Bar was still crowded when they left but Edwina noticed that Eric and the blond girl had disappeared.

"I've enjoyed this enormously," the columnist said as he shook hands with both of them. "Tell Dr. Rifkin he should always send his capable assistant in his place."

Capable? Edwina almost giggled. She had hardly said a word in the entire two hours except, "What will you have to drink?" and "Check please."

Because Señora Gomez seemed so helpless on the streets of New York, Edwina offered to take her by taxi to the apartment in Greenwich Village where she was staying with her sister.

"I appreciate your thoughtfulness more than I can say," the author assured her, as they rode down Fifth Avenue. "You have no idea how I felt when Dr. Rifkin wrote me he was lining up interviews for me here. I had always thought of publicity as something dreadfully vulgar and I had no idea what I would be called on to do. There was one photographer the other day who wanted me to jump in the air and throw dollar bills around to show how excited I was when I got the Blue Star money. But Mr. Bloch squelched him properly. For the rest it has been fun. I thought I would be struck dumb when I had to appear on Helen Hogan's radio program. The idea of talking in front of hundreds of people I couldn't even see was appalling. But we had a little chat before the microphone was turned on about my living in Mexico, so that when I was on the air I knew exactly what I was going to say. She had me sandwiched between a tap dancer and the woman president of a department store—wasn't that wonderful?"

"Tell me about your other interviews," Edwina encouraged her. She knew very well what they had been, but liked to get the Señora's refreshing version.

"Yesterday, Dr. Rifkin took me to lunch with Natalie Forbes, who is a food editor on one of the women's magazines. All we did was to exchange recipes. She's an enormously fat woman, you know, who must adore to eat.

Next year she's coming down to Mexico on vacation to stay at our inn. She said the fact that she would talk about it in her column would mean a lot of extra guests. If this keeps up we'll have to build a new wing. But I'll tell you something funny. I don't think any of these people have read my book, though Dr. Rifkin told me they all got advance copies. At least none so far has asked me any questions about it."

"I've read it," Edwina was able to say. "I thought it was lovely. It told me more about Mexico and its people than any book I've ever seen."

The author was delighted as a child at this, and before Edwina deposited her in front of her sister's apartment house, she too had an invitation to stay at the Buena Vista in Mexico. "Thank you," she said, smiling, "but I have to conquer America first."

She took a subway home then, her purse thin by this time.

Her aunt was dressed in street clothes just ready to go out.

"I had the most interesting afternoon, Margaret!" Edwina fairly exploded. "I took one of our writers to the Knowlton Towers for cocktails. . . ."

"Wasn't that nice?" Her aunt's voice showed her mind to be on other matters. "I wish I had time to hear all about it. I have to meet Bobbie at a new Armenian restaurant. Afterwards we're going to a Cinema 16 film showing of some early Russian movies. It should be fascinating. I do wish you could go too, but Bobbie only has one spare ticket. We'll see if we can get an extra one for you, if you like."

"Thank you, Margaret, but I'm exhausted. I think I'll go to bed early."

After her aunt had gone she changed to a housecoat and wandered listlessly around the apartment.

All her aunt's friends had nicknames like Judy or Bea or Lee, which made them sound like teen-age sorority girls, but they were all of mature years and responsible positions. Bobbie, for instance, was actually Barbara Knight, thin and gray-haired, the personnel manager for the Dorft Cheese Corporation.

Margaret's invitations to join them in their evenings out, kindly meant and never insistent, had come to represent a threat to Edwina, as though if she once accepted she would be doomed forever to all-feminine companionship. Still, staying home alone every evening could be dreary.

The phone rang, and she had a sudden irrational hope. She knew only one person who would be entertained and interested at hearing about her afternoon with the Señora and Max Deerfield. She hadn't seen Harry Dawes since their day in the park, and so far as she knew he didn't even have her telephone number. Nevertheless, she didn't try to analyze why, ever since that day, she had palpitations of the heart at the ring of the telephone.

But the voice on the wire was not Harry's.

"Hi, Edwina. Don't you recognize me any more? It's Matt."

"Matt, how are you?" She kept her voice cordially distant.

"I'm in your neighborhood," he said. "I thought you might like to take a walk with me or go somewhere. I have some big news for you."

"I'm much too lazy to get myself dressed all over again," she told him. "Come on up for a few minutes if you like. Margaret is out and I'll keep the Limoges china out of reach."

She had missed him, she realized, when he came in the door, big and lumbering.

"You're looking swell," he said, as he took a seat gingerly on the edge of the chaise longue, far from anything breakable.

"And you look prosperous." She noted a new suit and a new pair of shoes. If what he had to say was that he had once more changed his mind, she wondered how she would react.

He didn't keep her in suspense long. "I just had dinner with Mr. Blanchard," he said. "You know, our president. At his house. I had to tell someone and you were the nearest since he only lives up the Drive a couple of blocks. A real snazzy place with windows over the Hudson. Edwina, look at me! I'm the new Eastern State Regional Director. A raise. A bonus. A future."

"Congratulations, Matt. That's simply wonderful." Her warmth was genuine.

"I can buy a boat, an automobile, move to a better apartment," he continued exultantly. "I can even get married. That is, if you want to."

She hadn't known what she was going to say and now she didn't know why she said it.

"What happened to the other girl?"

"What other girl?"

"The one you left me for a few weeks ago."

He blinked his eyes in bewilderment, then let out a deep

breath. "Oh, her. That didn't last. You won't hold it against me?"

She shook her head, feeling very old and wise. It was all startlingly clear, as though lightning had illuminated a darkened landscape. "No, Matt, I won't hold it against you. There will be another girl coming along pretty soon but it won't be me."

"What makes you say that?" he demanded sullenly.

"I can't tell you." How could she say what she now realized about him—the big football hero who would for many years to come be looking for new conquests in which he could, temporarily at least, see the admiration that had been his during his college days? In between such conquests, he might always come back to her—that is, if she allowed it. Even married to him, it would be the same thing. She did not want that.

"I still will be friends with you, Matt. Let's settle for that."

"I'll never meet another girl like you, Edwina."

"Nonsense," she said. "Now, let's talk about something more interesting. Like Blanchard Service, for instance. You know, I've been thinking a lot about your company lately. It seems to me that what you need is a good publicity firm, like Robert Pritchard and Associates, so that the name of Blanchard would become known to all the small businessmen throughout the nation. How's that?"

In spite of himself, Matt burst out laughing. "I have to hand it to you the way you can change the subject."

"I'm serious," she protested, though laughing herself. "Blanchard is a natural for a publicity campaign. Everyone says so."

"I'll remember you for this," he said in high good humor. "I come up to ask you to marry me and you try to sell me a bill of goods on publicity."

"That's right." She rose, pulling him to his feet. "I'm purely a career girl now."

"You think you are? That I don't believe." He released his hands and suddenly he had his arms tightly around her and was reaching for her lips. "Career girls have no right to be so attractive," he murmured.

"Matt!" With more strength than she realized she had, she wrenched herself free from him. "What's got into you?"

"You. I don't want to lose you." He tried to embrace her again.

"You want everything, don't you?" she asked, eluding him. "You were the one who made the decision, Matt. Now you can live up to it."

He didn't believe her. "A man can always change his mind, can't he?" he demanded—and tried to approach her once more.

This time she gave him such a push that he stumbled against Aunt Margaret's sandalwood table, brushing from it a Venetian glass ashtray which fell to the floor and cracked in two.

Edwina and Matt both stared at the damage in horror.

"I did it again," Matt said sheepishly. "I guess you're right about me, Edwina. I'm a clod. I'm sorry. I apologize."

"Don't worry," she said, going to the door with him. "I'll tell Margaret I did it." She added as she held the door firmly open, "Best of luck to all my successors."

Once more he said as he left, "The thing about you, Edwina, is that you have class."

Somehow it didn't irritate her in the least. I know what it means now to exorcise a ghost, she thought just before she went to sleep. She felt fine.

The next morning Edwina asked Anna to show her how to fill out an expense-account slip.

"Here's one Eric just gave me." Anna picked the top one from a pile she kept in her desk fastened with a paper clip. "Make yours out the same way."

Edwina glanced at it. "For cocktails with Sid Randolph, managing editor of *Business News*. At Sherry Netherland. $13.50."

"Eric wasn't at the Sherry Netherland yesterday!" she burst out. "He was at the Knowlton Towers—with a blond girl who certainly wasn't Sid Randolph."

Anna pursed her lips. "Oh, he went to the Sherry Netherland later. The girl . . . he told me . . . a friend of his mother's he had to take out."

The plump blonde certainly didn't look like a friend of someone's mother any more than she looked like Sid Randolph. People say how blind love can be, she reflected, casting a pitying glance at Anna.

Max Deerfield's story on Señora Gomez' book, *The Way In*, and its charming author, came through a couple of weeks later. It was a beautiful story except for one thing. It neglected to mention that the book was a choice of the Blue Star Book Club.

"You didn't remind him of that?" Dr. Rifkin questioned Edwina, after he had seen the story.

She shook her head. "I didn't think of it. I'm so sorry."

"It's my fault," he said. "I should have told you. But after this, you will remember, won't you, that an essential of publicity is getting your product mentioned?"

"I'll remember it till the day I die," she promised fervently.

Chapter 9

Of the several accounts which the Pritchard office handled, Edwina knew least of all about the Golden Arrow Bus Lines. Though Eric had the title of account executive for this company, he was still as far as Edwina could tell resting on the laurels he had attained through the feature story in his father's magazine *Fact*. Since then fewer clippings came in mentioning Golden Arrow than for any other account, and most they did see originated in the company's home office in Philadelphia.

"What on earth do you do with yourself all day, Eric?" she asked him one morning when as usual he was loafing around the water cooler and trying to fluster Anna. "I've yet to see you working."

"I've learned a trick or so from Odell," he said defensively. "If you make work of publicity you never get anywhere."

"When you know as much as he does, you can afford to take it easy." She turned back to her own work.

"You're getting as bad a disposition as Dorothea," he

persisted. "What gives you the right to jump on me all the time?"

"I'm not jumping on you," she told him over her typing. "I'm just telling you for your own good."

"I think you two should stop fighting," Anna burst in.

"Edwina started it. I come in for a few moments of peace and quiet and she snaps my head off."

"I'm sure Edwina didn't mean anything," Anna defended her. "She was just trying to be helpful. Weren't you, Edwina?"

"She wishes she had my job," Eric offered. "She thinks she could handle it better than I can."

Edwina stopped her typing. "I couldn't do a worse job. That's for sure."

"And what would you do, Miss Know-it-all, to make people ride buses when airplane travel is practically as cheap and inestimably faster?"

"Buses are much cheaper than airplanes," she contradicted him. "You wouldn't know it but there are thousands of people who ride buses who can't afford airplanes. That's not the point. You can't make people want to ride on buses by telling them it's cheap. You have to convince them of the other advantages. That they'll see the country. That buses are comfortable, even luxurious. That buses are the safest way to travel."

He looked at her with grudging admiration. "How'd you think all that up on the spur of the moment?"

"It's obvious. Any beginner could do as well." She saw no reason for letting him know she'd been studying other bus lines' publicity and devoted a lot of mental energy to just how Golden Arrow should be publicized.

"I'll tell you what I'll do," he said. "I'll show you some

of the promotion stuff the company keeps sending me and let you see what you can do with it. I'm naturally doing this just as a special favor to you. I'd get in trouble if anyone knew it."

"The magnanimity of your offer overwhelms me," she said, resuming her typing. "No, thank you. I have my own job."

When he had gone Anna came over to her desk. "What made you talk to Eric like that, Edwina? It isn't like you."

"I'm sorry," Edwina said. "I guess I am getting to be like Dorothea. 'Everything for the good of the company.' "

"Oh, but I think you're right." Anna's voice was low and earnest. "Eric . . . does need someone to prod him once in a while. I've been worried about him too. It would be tragic if he should lose that account."

"He can't get away with what he's been getting away with forever," Edwina said with a shrug.

"Edwina . . ." Anna hesitated. "Would you do it? I mean, write some stories or something for the newspapers for him?"

"That isn't the way to make a man of him, Anna, and you know it," Edwina said softly. "People make good when they accomplish things on their own."

"If you get him started, maybe he'll want to try harder himself. Please, Edwina . . ." Anna pleaded.

"I'll go in and talk with him," Edwina promised finally. "But I don't think anything will come of it."

"I'll never be able to thank you enough," Anna said.

As a junior executive, Eric had the smallest office at Pritchard, no larger than a monk's cell. Edwina, seeing it for the first time, even felt a wave of understanding that he would want to come out once in a while and stretch his legs. But her sympathy vanished when she saw he was reading a racing sheet.

"I've decided to take you up on your offer," she announced coolly. "Give me what material you have and I'll see what I can make of it." She added, "I'm not doing it for you. I'm doing it for Anna, who seems to have more faith in you than your own mother."

He grinned up at her cockily. "That's mighty square of you. Here you are." He indicated a mass of papers on his desk.

"What do you do—just let them accumulate?" she demanded as she gathered them up as best she could. It seemed incredible that Mr. Pritchard would allow such inefficiency to continue, no matter who the youth's father was.

"I'd have to move out myself if I did that," he said in the same arrogant tone. "Every two months I sweep them all into the wastebasket. You're saving me that trouble."

"You're not worth it," she retorted as she marched out.

She had a busy evening ahead of her.

Margaret was out, fortunately. Edwina spread on the kitchen table the brochures, folders, photographs and memos that made up the mass of material Eric had turned over to her, going through them as she munched the cold chicken her aunt had left in the refrigerator. Many of the items, which would have made good news stories had they been released on time, were already out of date. She put them in a pile of discards. Some of the stories the material suggested would be good later on, and she put them aside too. There were two she felt were timely, one about a cross-country tour the Golden Arrow Line was sponsoring for a group of foreign students, and another on way stations which the line was inaugurating, similar to the old stagecoach inns, where bus passengers could relax for a few hours or a night, and enjoy local scenery and sometimes swimming or fishing. Happily the company photographer had taken some good pictures of both foreign students and the way stations.

That much decided, she retired to her own room with her portable typewriter, directing the first story to feature desks and the second to travel editors. In spite of the lack of enthusiasm with which she had tackled the job, once she got started she found herself excited. The old thrill she had felt doing stories for the college newspaper or for her father returned to her. Still, the results did not satisfy her when she read them over. There seemed something amateurish about her efforts, she could not say what.

It was no use. The editors had been right when they said she was too inexperienced to write for New York newspapers. Whatever had made her think she was capable of being a publicity writer?

A light knock at her door interrupted her brooding. "Edwina, are you still up? I saw your light. I've made some hot chocolate."

She hadn't even heard her aunt come in.

"I'll be right out, Margaret."

Margaret had had another absolutely fascinating evening, she told Edwina as she sipped her chocolate. A new play by Tennessee Williams. As her aunt chatted on about this and about Sue, the lovely woman friend who had gone with her, Edwina hardly listened. She had suddenly realized what was wrong with her stories. They were too feminine. Feminine writing was all right for fashions and food, but not for buses. "Excuse me, Margaret," she said, gulping the last of her chocolate. "I've got to get back to work."

She tried the stories again, this time deliberately using a crisper, harder style, at the same time striving to keep her initial enthusiasm. She still wasn't sure they were right when she had finished, but they were better at least. They were the best she could do.

She turned the two of them over to Eric in the morning. He looked at them cynically, made no comment, but passed them on to Anna to make clean copies. Edwina was in Mr. Odell's office taking dictation when he brought them in. It was one of Mr. Odell's duties to approve everything the junior executive turned out—an assignment that had given him no pain up to the present.

"I've decided to turn over a new leaf, Jeff," Eric announced. "Here are two stories for you—one for feature desks and one for travel editors."

Mr. Odell raised his eyebrows in disbelief, then read over the stories, making a few penciled changes as he did so.

"What have you been doing, Eric lad, taking a course in journalism?" he demanded when he was through. "There's nothing wrong with these. Get some more prints of the pictures and shoot them out."

"Glad you like them," Eric said with a wink at Edwina as he swaggered away.

"I didn't think he had it in him," Odell commented to Edwina.

She said nothing. It surprised her how much it went against the grain to see Eric casually accept credit for work that had cost her a night's sleep.

Nevertheless she kept on working up more stories about

Golden Arrow in her evenings at home. She didn't do it for Eric, nor was it, she admitted to herself, solely for Anna. Actually she was doing it for herself, to get the practical experience she knew she needed so badly. Some of the stories clicked, some of them missed. But when they were wrong, she had the opportunity of learning, through Mr. Odell's criticism to Eric, just what the matter was.

The only person outside of Anna to whom she confided what she was doing was Harry Dawes. After a long interval he had finally called her for lunch. They now had established this as a regular practice at least twice a week, not in the exclusive Château Rouge but in a modest Italian restaurant on 59th Street. Though the food was good and the prices moderate, it was rarely crowded. They had a table in the back which the waiter seemed to keep vacant specially for them.

Edwina could hardly believe she had once been tongue-tied in Harry's presence. Now her strictly limited one-hour lunch period never seemed enough for all the things they had to talk about.

He was intrigued by her efforts to save Eric his account, but did not approve.

"It's a waste of time. You won't get any thanks for it."

"I'm learning," she protested.

"Rot!" he exploded. "You know plenty already. All you lack is self-confidence."

"I suppose you think I can get myself a pair of glasses like yours and go out and get myself hired as publicity director for Pierce-Arrow Sales Corporation or Elizabeth Arden or somebody," she retorted. "Well, I can't. I've still a long way to go."

"You have to make the break sometime," he said, more quietly. "And as for this Eric, I don't think I'd trust him."

"I don't. The trouble is Anna is in love with him. And she shouldn't be."

"Why shouldn't she be?" he asked, suddenly serious.

She hadn't intended to tell even him, but she found herself blurting out the whole story—about Eric's borrowing money from her and, she was sure, from Anna, how peculiar this was in view of his alleged wealth, about the blond girl at the Knowlton, and Anna's defense of him in face of all the facts.

"I like it less and less," he said.

Their conversations were by no means limited to Anna and Eric. Much of the time they talked about themselves. Edwina learned to her surprise that Harry, who could look like the acme of the sophisticated New Yorker when he saw fit, had actually come from a working-class background. His father, a laborer in a New England textile factory, had died in a mill accident. His mother had insisted that part of the resulting compensation money must go to her eldest son's college education, so he would escape the privations they had known. There was still a younger brother in high school. Edwina deduced that part of the salary Harry drew went toward keeping him.

Strange as it was to think of "G. Harrison Dawes" coming from a poor family, it explained not only his drive to achieve a modicum of success without wasting time, but also his unconventional attitude toward art at the Metropolitan, so refreshingly different from that of many "cultured" people, whose culture consisted of being taught what they should and should not like.

That he had acquired his education the hard way was also a clue to why he seemed so much more of a person than Eric, though they were about the same age. The odd thing was that Harry never mentioned anything about his present personal life.

For herself, Edwina told him everything—about her childhood in Dantonville in the one-story white frame house furnished every-which-way, about her father's ambition to make his newspaper a crusading vehicle which would tell the truth to people, and how this sometimes made him unpopular with the local politicians and certainly kept him from making money; about her gentle Norwegian-born mother; about her little sister Doris, who was such a ladylike child compared to the tomboy Edwina had been; about old Judge Nordstrom and his memoirs; and about her own college life in a co-educational state university.

But somehow she never could get herself to talk about Matt and what had happened between them. Some reserve seemed to keep both of them from intruding a private life into their precious luncheons together. For Edwina sensed that these luncheons had come to mean as much to him as they did to her. When occasionally some last-minute task made her late, she would see him half a block away, standing restlessly in front of their restaurant, taking frequent glances at his watch as though he couldn't bear to see even a single minute make its escape without her arrival.

Whatever they talked about, they always came back to their mutual interest in publicity. He loved to discuss his different accounts with her. She became familiar with the varying techniques of promoting a night club, a ballet

111

school, and Swedish glass imports. If he realized he had become one of those persons who had "time and inclination to answer questions," he didn't kid her about it. He seemed to want her to know as much about publicity as he did.

One noon he greeted her with a wide grin. "Remember your idea for the Rierdon Soap Company holding an employee tea party?"

"It was *our* idea," she reminded him.

"No mind," he went on. "It's all set. The new publicity man over at the Association to Aid Fatherless Children is arranging the guest list. The Gold Rush entertainers are donating their services to sing western and folk songs. Best of all, Arlene Dare has consented to put in a personal appearance at the soap factory where she had her first job. Amazingly, she's agreed to make the collection speech for the children. I want you to talk to Odell about the tea angle. You should get some credit."

But she obstinately refused. "I have to stay out of the picture. Mr. Pritchard thinks a woman who dabbles in publicity is a monster. Until I'm ready to make a break I don't want him to know anything."

"I think you're being foolish," he said. "It's not going to hurt you if Pritchard realizes you're thinking in his interest. You've reached the stage where you could go out any day and get a job on your own."

Though he didn't succeed in changing her mind about the Rierdon party, she went back to the office in an exuberant mood.

"You look glowing," Anna commented when she came in.

"I feel glowing," Edwina said. "I feel as though I were

112

walking on air." She went to the window and threw it open, letting in a chill November gust.

"Oh dear," Anna protested, shivering. "It should be easy to walk on air like this. It's frozen solid."

"I'm sorry." Edwina closed the window again. She looked at her friend closer. "Anna, is something the matter?"

"Nothing new." Anna gave a sad smile. "It's just that there are some people born to be happy, like you, and others, like me, who always attract sorrow."

"It's Eric again, isn't it?" Edwina demanded angrily. "What's he done now?"

"He's a good person at heart," Anna said, evading her question. "But it's hard for him because he's always been accustomed to have everything."

"How can you deceive yourself so?" Edwina cried out. "Anna, I'm going to ask you something. Has Eric ever done one little thing for you?"

"Yes," Anna said, "he's made me feel alive. Most men pass me by as though I didn't even exist."

"Nonetheless Eric is not worth your little finger," Edwina asserted. "You'd make a wonderful wife for some man if you could only get him out of your system."

"Please don't talk like that," Anna said, tears filling her eyes. "I won't listen to you." She jumped from her desk and fled from the room, holding her handkerchief to her face.

Edwina started to go after her, then decided not to. It was perhaps better to let her cry it out by herself. Whatever the matter was, she reproached herself for being so blunt. Why make her feel any worse than she did? She stopped to pick up a slip of paper that had blown from

Anna's desk, started to replace it, then looked at it more closely. The paper was a note from a bank, saying they would agree to give her the loan she had requested.

She saw it all clearly. Eric had finally exhausted Anna's poor savings and had now persuaded her to take out a loan for him. What a rat he was! She gritted her teeth as she sat down at her own desk to start in on her first chore of the afternoon—pasting up clippings sent in as a result of her stories for the Golden Arrow Bus Lines.

Chapter 10

Edwina had dreaded her first Christmas in New York away from home. As the holidays approached her melancholy increased at the thought of a lonely dinner with Margaret, or if, as seemed likely, Margaret were invited out, by herself. She hadn't seen Matt again, and her meetings with Harry were still limited to lunches. Not that she spent all her evenings at home any more. A few suitors had sprung up: a nephew of one of Margaret's friends, a rather affected young man who took her out on occasion to art openings or concerts; a brother of one of her college girl friends who was working on Wall Street and whose interests were limited to stocks and bonds; a few others she had met in various ways. None of them really interested her and none seemed a suitable companion for the Yuletide season.

She was all the more delighted when around the middle of December she received a note from her father saying that the family had decided to pay a visit to New York to see how she was getting along, arriving the weekend before Christmas and staying until New Year's.

She met them at Grand Central and they looked so good to her she almost cried. Her mother was plump and red-cheeked and smiling and shy, as she remembered her, but with a few more gray strands in her blond hair. The furrows in her father's forehead and on each side of his mouth seemed to have deepened, but his deep-set blue eyes were as kindly and keen as ever. Doris, who was ten now, was still spindly, her curls tight as corkscrews. During the taxi drive uptown she sat stiff and straight in her new coat with fur on the collar, her eyes wide with wonder.

Margaret, who never did anything by halves, had a Christmas tree all silver and pink; the entire apartment was adorned with mistletoe and holly, and the fireplace filled with long-needled firs.

What a lot there was to talk about! All that had happened in Dantonville since Edwina had left was of interest to Margaret too, for Dantonville was also her home town.

The apartment was too small to sleep them all. Doris shared Edwina's bed, but Margaret had rented a room in a nearby hotel for Mr. and Mrs. Fiske, a wonderful treat for Edwina's mother who had never stayed in a hotel before—who, in fact, had not left Illinois since her parents had brought her there from Norway as a small child.

The day before Christmas, while Edwina was taking dictation from Dr. Rifkin, he remarked rather forlornly that this was no time of the year for an old bachelor like himself. Edwina found herself inviting him to Christmas dinner to meet her family, an invitation he accepted with alacrity.

Christmas began early with stockings full of presents dangling from the fireplace—Mrs. Fiske had seen to that, though in her own country it was wooden shoes that had

116

to be filled. After an elaborate breakfast there were more presents under the Christmas tree. Margaret, with Edwina's help, insisted on preparing the dinner. Mrs. Fiske for once in her life was commanded to sit quietly with her hands folded. She objected vociferously at first but finally decided she liked it.

Edwina's invitation to Dr. Rifkin proved an inspiration. He fitted in perfectly with the famly group, adding just the right touch of a new personality. He and Mr. Fiske got along famously, with their common interest in literature and current social conditions. But the most amazing thing was the attention the ex-professor paid to Margaret. Not only did he find her a fabulous cook, whose turkey excelled any he had ever tasted, but he seemed astounded at her ability to discuss pre-Columbian musical instruments, Haitian music, Japanese architecture, and even the nervous system of invertebrates. "It's a treat to meet a woman who is both an intellectual and a homemaker," he kept saying. Under his admiration, Edwina saw her aunt transformed from a frustrated dilettante spinster into an attractive and gracious hostess.

In the week that followed Edwina had ample time to get reacquainted with each member of her family. On Saturday morning she took Doris to the Museum of Natural History, sure-fire entertainment for any child, she thought. But Doris was only mildly interested in the dinosaurs and the mountain folk of Peru where records of South American birdcalls play continuously. She was much more excited by the display of famous jewels. After lunch, she asked Edwina to take her over to Fifth Avenue so she could see the pretty clothes in the windows of Bergdorf Goodman and Hattie Carnegie. Incomprehensible as it was to Edwina that a child of ten from Dantonville should know about Bergdorf Goodman and Hattie Carnegie, she enjoyed the afternoon "doing" the big Fifth Avenue shops almost—but not quite—as much as her little sister.

In the evenings after the others had gone to bed, Edwina had long talks with her father, mostly about her job and what she was trying to do. Only to her mother did she talk about more personal matters—about what had happened with Matt and about the young man she had lunch with frequently whom she found nicer than anyone she had ever met.

On New Year's Eve Dr. Rifkin invited them all down to his bachelor apartment to a buffet supper prepared by his housekeeper. It was the sort of place Edwina would have imagined for him, lined from floor to ceiling with books, but with the furniture shaky and in disrepair, and papers piled everywhere. Margaret was so distressed at this disorder that she impulsively suggested the professor should come up and have dinner with them at least once a week, to get away from it all, and he said nothing would please him more. The next day the family took a train back to Dantonville.

Their departure left Edwina empty and lost. She was certain now she would never be able to adjust permanently to living without a family, as Margaret had done. She got over her momentary depression by plunging into her office duties.

After Señora Gomez there had been other Blue Star authors and books to work on—an English novelist whose latest book was set in the turbulent Middle East; a novel by a Portuguese writer about a family of emigrants in Brazil; a book by an atomic scientist about the potentials of atomic power for peacetime progress (one of the few that warranted a press conference and front-page coverage).

The book column for weekly newspapers was a reality now. Mats and mimeographed sheets were sent out regularly to newspapers who had requested this service, and judging from the stacks of clippings that poured in they were well received. To Edwina's disappointment an outside writer had been hired to prepare these columns; it was an assignment she would have loved herself, but had not dared ask for.

Dr. Rifkin had another project on the fire now—a monthly prepared lecture on current books to be sent out to the thousands of women's clubs throughout the country. Edwina had worked with him closely, tracing the lists of such clubs and sending out the initial inquiries to them, as they had done with the weekly newspapers.

"How would you like to try your hand at one of these scripts when we get under way?" he asked her one morning. "You could use the same sort of thing that appears in the newspaper columns, only with a little more detail about Blue Star books and authors. It shouldn't be hard for you; you know what women like to hear, I'm sure."

"I'd love it," she told him, utterly delighted. Had Margaret mentioned to him her thwarted ambitions or had he just figured it out for himself? She didn't question her good fortune.

She told Harry about her possible new assignment at lunch that day. He had been away over the holidays, taking his vacation to visit his own family, and so she had not seen him for several weeks.

"Fine," he said. "At least this will be on the up-and-up —something you'll have to be given credit for."

She also told him about her latest effort on behalf of the Golden Arrow Bus Lines. Eric had received a note from the home company that one of their drivers, a man named Joseph Greenspan, would soon have completed thirty years in their service without a preventable accident—a wonderful record. Edwina had proposed they make a big affair of it, hold a ceremonial dinner with Mr. Greenspan as the guest of honor, inviting members of the National Safety Council, of the Motor Vehicle Department, perhaps some doctors or psychologists who gave tests to the company driver applicants. Eric had passed her suggestion on to Odell as coming from himself. Odell was all for it.

But Harry was less enthusiastic about this. "I think you should forget about Golden Arrow and let Eric stumble on to his own downfall. You're working up a dead end street."

"I can't give it up," Edwina said stubbornly. "Anna would be brokenhearted."

She was very busy at the office these days and one reason was that Jeff Odell was giving her more and more responsibility. She wrote many of his letters now, based on his cryptic notes, and frequently made telephone calls for him. He let her do the final polishing of his news stories and prepare them for the mimeograph company. When stories with a woman's angle were required, he encouraged her to make first drafts of them for his editing. "I never was able to think like a woman," he explained, as though some apology were necessary for passing this task on to her.

But Edwina was too pleased with her more varied work program to notice anything out of the ordinary in his requests.

One morning when he had called her in as usual to have coffee with him, Dorothea happened to walk in with a memo from Mr. Pritchard. She looked at the coffee cartons, at Edwina sitting in apparent idleness with her notebook closed.

"This office is supposed to promote tea, Mr. Odell," she said icily. "How would it look if Mr. Blakeley of the Tea Conference Board should walk in and see you drinking coffee?"

Mr. Odell grinned at her. "He'd probably think it a big joke."

But the incident made Edwina uncomfortable and after that she told him not to order any more coffee for her in the mornings, that it was bad for her nerves.

A few days later Patricia Evarts suggested they have lunch together. This was unusual, for Pat had a string of boy friends and frequently boasted she never had to pay for her own lunch or dinner.

"I wanted to talk to you about something I didn't dare say in the office, Edwina, honey," she said, as they sat opposite each other in a booth in the crowded coffeeshop. "It's about Mr. Odell. He's such a nice man. I think he's in danger. I think they're planning to fire him."

"It can't be true! They wouldn't do that! He's been there for years," Edwina gasped all in one breath.

Pat nodded. "I just happened to overhear a conversation." No one in the office ever pressed Pat on how she "just happened" to overhear conversations.

But this time Edwina was too concerned to care about ethics. "Just what was the conversation?"

"I think Dorothea's back of it," Pat said cryptically. "I don't think she likes his coming in later than the others and leaving early, even though Mr. Pritchard agreed to it. She thinks it's bad for the morale of the office. And now I think she thinks he's getting too old to carry on."

"It's not so!" Edwina protested indignantly against all these "I think" and "she thinks." "He not only does all his own work but he supervises Eric Kingston's work as well and occasionally helps out Dr. Rifkin. Who was Dorothea talking with? How much influence does she have?"

"I just know what I know," said Pat. "I thought maybe you could warn him."

Try as she would, Edwina couldn't get any more out of her.

As a result of the receptionist's hints, she redoubled her efforts to take work from Mr. Odell's shoulders so there could be no complaints against their department. In spite of her protestations to Pat, there were things that bothered her. Sometimes in the middle of telling her something, Odell would stop abruptly as though his mind were far away. Sometimes, too, he would forget the name of a newspaper person he knew intimately and Edwina would have to fill the gap.

There was nothing wrong, however, in the way he organized the ceremonial dinner in Philadelphia for Joe Greenspan, the Golden Arrow bus driver with his splendid thirty-year safe-driving record. Mr. Odell planned everything, but, to Edwina's delight, saw to it that Eric worked harder than he ever had done in carrying out the "Jimmy Higgins" work, even sending him off to Philadelphia for the occasion. Since the Golden Arrow was a member of the National Safety Council, their drivers were eligible for the Council's safe driving awards. A Council member presented Joe with his at the dinner, after which the driver made a one-sentence speech in which he modestly attributed his accomplishment to "good luck and good health." Newsreel and TV cameras recorded both the giving of the award and the driver's speech. Local press coverage was excellent and the Associated Press sent out a syndicated story across the country. As an aftermath, Joe was invited to appear on several other TV and radio programs. A renowned psychiatrist made a statement, also syndicated, advocating setting up higher standards for all applicants for driving licenses to conform with those set by Golden Arrow.

Though Eric could truthfully claim only a small share in this success, Edwina had to admit he had not done badly. Anna, of course, was delighted, convinced that the young man had reformed.

With all the resulting publicity from this and the other stories on behalf of Golden Arrow, an unforeseen thing happened. The company decided not to renew their contract with Pritchard, not because they were dissatisfied—in fact, their compliments about the magnificent job that had been done were fulsome—but simply because business was so good that for the present they felt no need for publicity other than what their regular staff could handle.

"You prodded me into action, all right," Eric told Edwina bitterly. "You prodded me right up and out of a job."

But he was not fired. With the discontinuance of the Golden Arrow account, Mr. Pritchard, impressed with recent activities, decided Eric was "too good a man to lose."

In the meantime the Rierdon Soap Company employee tea charity, twice postponed because of Arlene Dare's delay in coming to New York, had been definitely set for the middle of February. A couple of weeks beforehand Harry made an appointment with Mr. Odell to discuss it. He had been in the office about five minutes when Mr. Odell rang for Edwina.

"I believe you have met my secretary, Edwina Fiske," he said as she came in.

"I have had that honor," Harry said, rising. "How are you, Miss Fiske?"

"I'm fine, thank you," Edwina answered. She felt herself blushing, for it seemed to her that Mr. Odell had seen through their subterfuge.

"Edwina is my right arm here," Mr. Odell continued with no hint of anything unusual. "Somewhat more, I should say, because she remembers all the things I forget, which a mere arm could never do. I want her to take some notes for us and in general listen in on this session so she'll know what it's about."

"Excellent," Harry commented, waiting for her to sit down next to her employer's desk before he resumed his own place.

For Edwina's benefit, Mr. Odell explained briefly the plan for the Rierdon charity tea. She noticed Harry looked uncomfortable during this. She had made him promise not to mention that she had any part in the affair, but she knew he didn't like it.

"In other words, this is a publicity 'tie-up' in the grand manner, Edwina," Mr. Odell was saying. "It involves the

124

charity, the Tea Conference Board, the Rierdon Soap Factory, not to mention Miss Arlene Dare and the other entertainers. But though we all have an interest in it, we must remember that it is essentially a plan to help the Association to Aid Fatherless Children. All releases must be prepared carefully so they do not sound as if we were doing this strictly for publicity."

"Do you think it would be a good idea to have all releases sent out from the Association offices?" Harry interpolated.

"By all means," Mr. Odell acquiesced, "though you should certainly work with the charity in writing them."

"What I'd like to suggest, sir, is that the Association and I do the first drafts of all releases and send them over to you for editing and revising," Harry said. "Your long experience will be invaluable to us."

Mr. Odell chuckled. "That's agreeable to me, so long as I don't have to sit down and compose them. I guess you know my reputation for laziness. Another thing—make sure that the advance stories stress that none of the guests is required to make a donation. People won't show up otherwise. Also that the affair is being sponsored by the employees of the Rierdon Soap Company rather than the company itself. That gives an unusual news angle."

"Good enough," said Harry.

"The Association has offices in other large cities, doesn't it?"

Harry nodded.

"They can take care of handling local publicity in those places much better than we can from here. You might suggest it to them."

"A good point." Harry made a note in a small book he

carried. His whole attitude was one of deferential respect for the older man's opinions, though Edwina knew he had had some of the same ideas himself.

They went on to discuss other tasks involved in staging such an affair—the drawing up of the invitations to the press as well as to various dignitaries and celebrities in the entertainment and sports world; the seating arrangements; hiring their own photographer to supplement the photographers that the newspapers might send; notifying the clipping services of the event; the scheduling of the program; the tea service.

The Tea Conference Board would donate the tea, Mr. Odell promised, though they would appreciate it if Mr. Blakeley, the Director of the Board, would be given thanks for this donation. The tea people would be glad to give all the help and advice they could in return for having tea mentioned in the various news stories, and for photo shots of celebrities drinking tea at the affair. . . .

It did not surprise Edwina that while her boss was generous in time and ideas, he left most of the routine work to Harry. There was no doubt in her mind now that fundamentally he was tired of his job. But if, as seemed likely now, he was to be discharged, what would happen to him? She knew he had a large house and family out in Long Island, and that like most men in "communications," he lived up to his income if not beyond it. How would he, at his age, get another job when he had to compete with younger, more energetic men?

The morning of the Rierdon affair, Odell had Edwina call up all the newspapermen he had personally invited.

"Most of them won't come," he told her. "It's not that much of a story. Still, they should be encouraged."

One of those she called was Max Deerfield, who remembered her and said he would do his best to be there —though he would be late since he had to be at the Stork Club at four to meet a celebrated lady anthropologist.

At noon Mr. Odell went down to the factory with Harry to make a final check on seating arrangements and tea service. He returned to the office a couple of hours later and immediately rang for Edwina. He looked tired.

"I'm not going back there," he informed her. "I have to take an early train. Pritchard is tied up with his air-conditioner executives. Edwina, I want you to go in my place. Mr. Blakeley of the Tea Conference Board will be there. First and foremost, see that he enjoys himself."

Ordinarily Edwina would have been enormously pleased. But for his sake she was worried.

"Couldn't you take a later train this one time? Mr. Pritchard might be annoyed if he thought I was the only one from here for such an important event."

"Let him be angry," Mr. Odell said shortly. "There's nothing more I can do." He added, as she sat in front of him wanting so much to speak more frankly, "Stop looking at me like that, young lady, as though I were deserting a sinking ship. The truth is I don't feel too well."

She didn't believe him, but there was nothing more she could do.

"Is there anything else I should do besides looking after Mr. Blakeley?"

"No. Dawes has everything in hand, and of course the Fatherless Children people will be there too. Just look pretty and be nice to everyone."

She started for the door, but he called her back.

127

"Oh, Edwina, one thing. I don't want you to go on thinking you've deceived me."

"About what?" She blanched, thinking maybe he had heard the rumors about him floating around the office.

"About Eric and his buses," he said. "I knew all the time you were writing stories for him."

"You did?" She stared at him, flabbergasted. "Who told you?"

"No one. I figured it out for myself. It was a matter of adding two and two. Eric couldn't have done those stories. You wanted to try."

She felt herself flushing. "You didn't tell Mr. Pritchard?"

He shook his head. "I might have if it had gone on much longer. I don't particularly like to see that type of exploitation. Sit down a moment. I think you should know what you've let yourself in for. First, I want to get one thing straight. Am I correct in my judgment that you didn't act out of any personal attachment to Eric? That your affections are more likely fixed on . . . well, on someone else?"

She could only nod.

"About Eric," he continued. "A year or so ago he ran up a lot of debts and forged some checks in his father's name to pay them. Women and gambling, I suppose. His real genius is throwing money around. Without it, he's lost. His father called him on the carpet, threatened him with jail if he ever tried anything like that, scandal or not, and ordered him out of the house for good, saying if he wanted to live he'd have to work. But then he got soft-hearted and went to Pritchard to persuade him to give Eric a job. When Pritchard stalled, Kingston senior went

128

one step further and put pressure on Golden Arrow to give their publicity account to Pritchard—on condition Eric be allowed to handle it. So Pritchard figured he had nothing to lose. But the boy would have been dropped from the payroll when Golden Arrow called quits if it hadn't been for you. Now he's the golden-haired boy." He smiled quizzically. "We'll have to see what happens in the next installment.

"Edwina, I want you to understand that at this point he probably won't have any affection for you. He's too much indebted to you. But if there should be any trouble, I want you to promise to come to me. Is it a deal?" The look he gave her was at once fatherly, solicitous and compassionate.

"I promise, Mr. Odell," she said. Inwardly she was thinking, poor Anna.

Chapter 11

"I want to welcome all of you today in the name of the Association to Aid Fatherless Children," the chairman of that Association, standing on the stage of the Rierdon Recreation Hall, began his address. Edwina, from her vantage point at the rear next the entrance, breathed a sigh of relief. The affair was finally under way.

The soap company recreation hall was large and rectangular, the walls painted a soft blue with contrasting red woodwork. Most of the time ping-pong and billiard tables lined one side; a TV corner was fixed up at one end; easy chairs and low tables were scattered around where employees could eat lunch, read, or talk. Sometimes, Harry had told Edwina while he was showing her around, dances were held here. At Thanksgiving and Christmas, turkeys were raffled off; it was here that the Company's Thespian Club put on amateur theatricals.

Today an employee committee had made it over into a gaily decorated teahouse, with Chinese lanterns hung along red and blue paper chains, and tables set with mats, each with a bouquet of fresh flowers. Between the tables waiters hired from a catering service moved by with pots of boiling water and trays laden with sandwiches and cakes. The tea served was a special blend prepared and donated by the Tea Conference Board; Edwina's last task before the program began was to check with the head-waiter to make sure all his men knew how to make it properly.

The guests of this affair were the patrons and friends and members of the Association—among them church leaders, outstanding educators, leaders in municipal politics and in business, society people, heads of unions, even a few foreign diplomats from the United Nations. The hosts—and this was the unique feature—were the Rierdon Soap Factory employees. Practically all of them had come, Edwina judged, dressed in their best: chemists, research workers, office workers, as well as skilled operators, warehousemen, packers, soap boilers, women who ran various machines or carried out more routine tasks. There were gnarled and rugged workmen and pretty young girls, smooth-faced boys and plain elderly women, people of different races and ancestry from many lands. They were seated at their own tables, and the thing Edwina noticed about them when she first came in was that they all seemed to be having a good time, talking, calling to each other, exchanging jokes and laughing —to a much greater degree, indeed, than their more distinguished-looking guests. But when the speaking started, they quieted down to a dead silence.

The hall was crowded by this time except for the press table, up near the front, which was still nearly empty. That was not surprising. Harry had told her that the press usually managed to miss the first and dullest part of any charity occasion.

The Association chairman, unperturbed by the flash of the press photographer's camera (who took pictures of each of the speakers as they appeared), continued with a few words about the history and aim of his organization, made his speech short from long experience, and turned the chair over to Mr. Rierdon, president of the Rierdon Soap Company, with a somewhat flowery introduction.

Mr. Rierdon, a gentle-looking old man with white hair and white mustaches, was greeted by a round of applause, most vociferous from the employee tables. His speech was short too, somber and somewhat sentimental, stressing how much it meant to him to have gathered before him the two groups of people who meant most to him— his friends and companions of the Association and the friends and companions of his small business. He in turn introduced the master of ceremonies, a comedian of some repute who was also a patron of the Association. As M.C. he presented with professional wit the first performer, a guitarist and singer of hobo songs from the Gold Rush night club.

It gave Edwina a thrill of satisfaction to remember that this impressive function had started from a germ of an idea—her idea, Harry insisted! There was something creative in this kind of publicity, a building of something tangible and real from a casual conversation. She looked around for Harry but could not see him; she judged he must be backstage with the performers. She noticed that several new guests had arrived, and slipped over to join the girl at the table by the door, whose job it was to take the name of each newcomer. One was a reporter from the *Times,* whom Edwina directed around the side of the hall to the press table. Another, she recognized from his picture, was the spare, bald-headed director of the Tea Conference Board, Mr. Blakeley.

"I was supposed to meet Jeff Odell here," he was saying to the girl, as he stared over the audience. "Have you any idea where the deuce he is?" The girl looked blank.

Edwina stepped forward. "I'm so sorry, Mr. Blakeley. Mr. Odell wasn't well and couldn't make it. I'm Edwina Fiske. May I find you a table?"

His reply was inaudible for the clapping—along with some stamping and cheering—that broke out at the end of the guitarist's first number. From the expression on the tea man's face, it was obvious that he was not content.

In her months at Pritchard, Edwina had picked up a few facts about him: that he was English-born, the youngest son of an English peer, who in accordance with the tradition of some such youngest sons had come to the New World to make his fortune. Unlike many of his kind, he had taken a fancy to American life and become a naturalized citizen. The one thing that had bothered him about his adopted country was that nobody could make a decent cup of tea. Tea should be strong and hot, a full teaspoon of tea leaves to each person, the water poured over the leaves at the moment it came to a boil. It should be allowed to steep at least three minutes and preferably five. The insipid stuff they served in American restaurants was enough to turn any man's stomach. That people should dip a tea bag into a cup of hot water for a few seconds and call it tea was beyond imagination. No wonder Americans sneered at the drink.

Over the years, the subject had become an obsession with him and had led eventually to his affiliating himself with the strictly American Tea Conference Board. For him the first job of the tea publicity campaign was to re-educate Americans in the manner of brewing tea. Once that was accomplished, he was certain that the prejudice against it would disappear of its own accord.

During the lull after the applause, Edwina repeated her question: "May I find you a table, Mr. Blakeley? The entertainment is just beginning. I'm sure you will enjoy it."

"Pardon me, who did you say you were?" he asked.

"Edwina Fiske. I work with Mr. Odell. He sent me to take care of you."

"He did?" He regarded her curiously and then seemed to decide to accept the situation. "That was thoughtful of him. I hate to come into places where I don't know anybody. Let's have some tea."

They sat at a small table at the back, not a good place to see the show but the best there was left. The guitarist sang an encore. He was followed by a solo by the star performer of the ballet school which was also one of Harry's accounts. This was followed by local talent: a short skit put on by the soap company's Thespian Club. It seemed very amusing from the way the audience laughed, but Edwina and Mr. Blakeley were too far away to judge. Their waiter was an unpardonably long time serving them. In between the acts, Edwina bravely kept chattering, explaining the work of the Association to Aid Fatherless Children, the unusually fine working conditions at the Rierdon Soap Company factory, remarking how nice it was of Miss Dare to contribute her time. But with all her efforts she could see that her companion was getting restless. He was at heart still an Englishman, and Englishmen want their tea when they want it!

Eventually the waiter came over to them with his tray. Then, before Edwina's shocked gaze he served them—with two teacups filled with water not even steaming, and tea bags at the side.

"Take them away," she ordered the waiter quickly, before Mr. Blakeley could speak. "I told the headwaiter myself. The tea must be served in a pot with boiling water poured over the tea leaves."

The waiter looked disgusted but with a brusque gesture he swooped up the teacups and departed with them.

"I don't know what happened, Mr. Blakeley. He must have been brought in late after the other waiters. They knew, I'm sure they did." Whatever she said, she felt that Robert Pritchard & Associates would have a black mark against them and that she would inevitably be blamed.

"Hrumpff." Her companion cleared his throat. "Are you sure that all these other people haven't been drinking this abominable stuff?"

"I'm sure," she told him. "I watched before the entertainment started. They carried around large teapots. Everything was going fine then."

"Hrumpff," he said again, and made no further remark until the waiter returned with more tea, correctly served.

He took a sip. "That's right. That's very good."

At that critical moment of test, Harry appeared beside them, an anxious look on his face. "Miss Fiske, I've been looking all over for you. Will you come with me, please?"

Why does he have to come now, she thought, just when things may go smoothly?

"Mr. Dawes, I want you to meet Mr. Blakeley, Director of the Tea Conference Board." She presented her companion.

"I'm delighted to meet you, sir." Harry held out his hand with his customary poise. "An emergency has arisen or I wouldn't take Miss Fiske away from you."

"I don't know anyone here," muttered Mr. Blakeley, accepting Harry's extended hand. "I don't like to be left alone when I don't know anybody."

"On second thought, would you come with us, sir?" Harry suggested. "It's a very delicate situation."

With a reluctant glance at his steaming tea, Mr. Blakeley rose. Edwina, mystified, went along as Harry, his expression strangely grim, led them out the rear door, up a flight of stairs to a door with the word *President* on it in gold letters, which he flung open.

Inside on a dark green leather settee sat a young woman, dressed exquisitely in a gown of some sheer gray material with long full sleeves and molded bodice. She had her hands to her face and she was sobbing. Even so, Edwina had no doubt that she was their star guest, the girl who, according to all the stories about her, really had been spotted by a movie scout in a drugstore as potential Hollywood material, and who had in a few brief years soared from wrapper in a soap factory to a movie glamour queen.

In front of her stood Mr. Rierdon, looking pained and bewildered. At her side was a nervous little man holding

136

a large pocket handkerchief as if he didn't quite know what to do with it.

"Honey, you've got to go on," he was saying. "You promised. You'll get a bad name with the press if you don't."

"I told you I won't. I can't." Arlene Dare resumed her sobbing.

"But why, Miss Dare?" Mr. Rierdon demanded plaintively. "What have we done?"

"Miss Dare, I've brought some friends to meet you," Harry said.

She looked up at him through her fingers. "Oh, it's you again," she said hostilely. "Go way."

For the first time since she had known him, Edwina saw Harry completely nonplused. He turned to her and Mr. Blakeley. "For some reason Miss Dare has decided she does not wish to appear. She will not explain her reasons to Mr. Rierdon or to her press agent or to me. I thought you might talk to her, Edwina."

Mr. Blakeley spoke up. "The young lady has an attack of nerves. What she needs is a good hot cup of tea. I will have the headwaiter make one for her. A cup of tea is the best thing in the world for nerves." He vanished.

"Pull yourself together, honey," the press agent pleaded. "It's nearly curtain call."

His weak attempt at humor fell flat and Miss Dare started to sob more audibly.

Impulsively Edwina knelt beside her. "Tell me what the trouble is," she said. "Maybe I can help."

Miss Dare took her hands from her eyes and looked down at her with swollen, tear-streaked eyes. "You have a nice face," she said unexpectedly. "I like you."

137

"That's my baby," exclaimed the press agent. "Let me dry your eyes." He flourished the handkerchief.

She glared. "I don't like you. You have no heart. Get out, all of you, and leave me with this nice girl."

Abashedly the three men filed out. Edwina sat down beside her. "There, there," she said consolingly, as though to a child who had hurt its finger. "Everything will be all right."

"You can't know." Miss Dare started sniffling again. "I can't go out there. I thought I could but I can't. There's someone . . . I just can't bear to see."

Instinct warned Edwina not to press her. "Do you know that everyone who works in this factory has been waiting a long time now, just to catch a glimpse of you? They feel you belong to them because you once worked here, and now you're famous, it makes them proud and happy as if your fame belonged to them too. It would be a pity to disappoint them."

She kept on talking in this vein while Arlene Dare watched her thoughtfully and suspiciously. "And the press?" she asked finally.

"The press isn't important," said Edwina. "Do as you like about them." At this moment it didn't strike her that this was an amazing statement to come from a publicity girl.

Miss Dare took a deep breath and suddenly her eyes sparkled with determination. "I'll go talk to them," she announced. "I will. Nothing is going to stop me . . . only, I feel so awful. . . ."

The door opened and in walked Mr. Blakeley, proudly balancing a cup of tea.

"Here you are, miss," he said cheerily. "Just what you need."

Miss Dare seized the cup avidly. "Wonderful," she said, taking a gulp. "Who is this nice man? I just love bald heads. They always make me want to go skating."

The implication was a little disrespectful but Mr. Blakeley was beaming.

"Mr. Blakeley, director of the Tea Conference Board," Edwina murmured. "Mr. Blakeley, Miss Arlene Dare."

"Enchanted," he said, taking her free hand and kissing it.

Edwina opened the door. Mr. Rierdon, the press agent, and Harry were standing just outside. "Everything's all right now," she told them. Seeing their worried faces, like fathers-to-be in a hospital waiting room, she could hardly repress a desire to add, "It's a boy."

"Whew," Harry breathed, as they walked away to leave Miss Dare a few moments to recuperate. "That was the worst fit of female temperament I ever met with."

"It wasn't just temperament," Edwina asserted. "She had a reason for not wanting to appear."

"She had?" Harry looked at her sharply. "What was it?"

Edwina shook her head. "I don't know. It's just a hunch." But she felt vaguely troubled.

Her fears were dissipated a little later when the star, introduced by Mr. Rierdon, stepped out onto the small stage, clear-eyed and self-possessed, to receive an ovation. How lovely she looked in her clinging gray dress, her dark hair loose around her shoulders, her make-up restored to perfection without a trace of her recent outburst.

The tables were all full now, and Edwina, with Mr. Blakeley, was standing at the rear along with other late arrivals. Miss Dare addressed them as though they were all guests in the intimacy of her own home.

"Friends and fellow workers," she began in her musical Hollywood-trained voice, and started by speaking of the days when she had put bars of soap into packing boxes for Rierdon Soap Company (her first job), how frightened she had been, and how she had gradually gained confidence because of the warmth and camaraderie of the others in the shop. They mustn't think she had forgotten them—John, Amy, Mabel, Morris—she pointed them out, asked them to rise, and laughed, delighted as a child at her feat of memory after nearly ten years away from them.

She swung quickly then into the matter that had brought them all together—their common desire to do something for the children who had no fathers and for their mothers who wanted to keep their young ones near them.

It was hard, she said, and she knew how hard, because she too had come from a family where one of the parents was missing. Only in her case it had been her mother who had died when she was small and her father had had to earn a living and at the same time try to give her a mother's care. Sometimes he had seemed too stern with her but now that she was older she appreciated all he had tried to do. Her heart went out to any child who had to get along without a father's love. She wanted to start the donations today by matching the first man who would offer a thousand dollar check for carrying out the work of the Association. . . .

"You, sir." She gestured toward one prosperous-looking gentleman at a table near the front, a bank executive Edwina knew from the guest list. But the bank executive looked down guiltily. The honor done him was not yet sufficient to open his pocketbook. She started all over again about the fine work done by the Association, and again made her offer and her appeal. Still no one responded.

What a thankless task she had! Edwina's sympathies were strong with this young woman, who had had this chore forced on her by her press agent, and who nevertheless was putting into it everything she had. Nor, in spite of the seeming indifference, was Edwina the only one with this reaction. At one of the tables in front of Edwina, where a group of men from the shop were sitting, there was a slight disturbance. An oldish fellow with close-cropped gray hair, muscular build, and the features of a stubborn Irishman, was trying to get to his feet and being restrained by his younger comrades. He pushed them aside and headed for the front of the hall.

"I'm bringin' you your thousand dollars, Mary," he boomed, brandishing a bankbook like a weapon. "You don't need to be askin' any of these stuffed shirts. It's to your own kin you should be turnin'."

The actress's deep blue eyes went wide and her face blanched. "Papa!" she cried out. "You shouldn't . . ."

Before the stunned audience could gasp for breath, he had leaped up on the stage beside her.

"My little girl! My little Mary!" He stared at her with something like awe, obviously impervious to the many eyes fixed on him.

A camera bulb flashed. The master of ceremonies tried

to intervene, but the old man pushed him aside as he had the young men at his table.

"I have something to say and I'm goin' to say it." He stepped to the front of the stage. "You down there," he shouted, waving his arm to encompass all of them, "I want you all to know this is my own little girl, Mary O'Hara, and that I'm the old fool who disowned her, thinkin' it was sinful her being on the stage. I ask you, if it was sinful, would she be up here pleading like an angel for those little fatherless waifs? No, it's a noble calling she had and it was I who was the sinful one ever to think anything different. And all of you," his voice roared out, "you should be ashamed of yourselves sittin' there like mummies while the sweet words pour from her that would be melting the stones. It's high time you started giving and I'm going to stay right up here and see that you do. You tell them, Mary."

"Yes, Papa." The film actress known to her public as Arlene Dare stepped up beside him. "My father, Michael O'Hara, a freezer operator at the Rierdon Soap Company for the past twenty years, has just given his life savings to help the Association to Aid Fatherless Children," she said quietly. "Who among you will match his gift?"

"I'll double it, young lady!" The voice was at Edwina's side and it was Mr. Blakeley's. "I give two thousand dollars in the name of the Tea Conference Board."

"Two thousand dollars from Mr. Walter Blakeley in the name of the Tea Conference Board," called out the master of ceremonies.

"The nice tea gentleman!" exclaimed Miss Dare, throwing him a kiss. "Now who will match his gift?"

Amid the general bedlam and uproar other bids followed in rapid succession. The ushers rushed back and forth bringing up checks and promissory notes. Then finally, with a short speech of gratitude from the Association president, it was all over. The guests straggled out, all except for a cluster of newspapermen around Miss Dare and her father.

Mr. Blakeley turned to Edwina. "A good show," he said. "Now let's see if we can talk the waiter into bringing us another cup of tea. I never did get to drink mine, you know."

Harry, who had been with the newspapermen, joined them presently at their table. His expression was awestruck. "Any reporter who thought this a gag changed his mind talking to Mike O'Hara," he said, sitting down heavily. "Even Mr. Rierdon had no idea he was Arlene's father. He brought her to work here so he could keep an eye on her, but didn't let on she was his daughter." He wiped his forehead with his handkerchief. "What do you think of it, Edwina?"

"At this stage I'm beyond thinking," she told him.

"I must congratulate you, young man," said Mr. Blakeley. "It was a good show."

"And that for an ex-Englishman is high praise," Harry remarked to Edwina, after they had found him a cab and waved him good-bye. He stood on the curb looking down at her with a mocking smile.

"I'd better be going," she said.

"Meeting your fiancé?"

"No," she admitted. "That is, not this evening."

"I thought you might come home to dinner with me.

143

If you're free. And if you don't mind a subway. Payday being tomorrow."

"I don't mind," she said.

On their way to the subway station, he stopped at an outside telephone booth. "Just a moment. I have to notify the family you're coming." He kept the door open as he called, and she heard him say, "She says yes." And after a pause. "In about ten minutes."

Chapter 12

Even from the outside the brownstone house before which
they stopped looked as though it had known better days.
The inside hallway with its scarred mahogany stand and
worn carpet was definitely shabby. Harry showed no embarrassment at the lack of elegance. "It's on the fourth
floor. I trust you have good lungs."

"Good enough," she said, though she was panting before they finished their climb.

There he knocked on a door three times, waited,
knocked three more times. It was flung open.

"Edwina! It's about time."

The speaker was a youth with a crewcut and healthy
coloring, dressed in a sport sweater and slacks. He seized
her hand and pulled her in.

"Here she is in the flesh, fellows."

Two other very young men, one with red hair and
freckles, the second with black hair and dark soulful eyes,
catapulted over to her.

"Welcome to the Outcasts of Fifty-Third Street," the
red-haired one greeted her.

"I'm glad to meet you, Edwina," said the youth with black hair, more formally. "We've heard an awful lot about you."

"How do you do?" murmured Edwina, more than a little overwhelmed at such a reception.

"We certainly have heard about you," echoed the boy who had opened the door. "Edwina, the most beautiful girl in New York . . . the cleverest publicity woman . . . the pleasantest . . . the gayest . . ." The words were a chant, interrupted by a seal-like bark as the dachshund, Dodo, waddled into the room and leaped up on her, wagging his tail.

"Quiet, please!" Harry raised his hand like a sergeant-at-arms, and for a moment even Dodo was silent. "Edwina, this is my family." He presented the three in the order of their first appearance: "Pud, Deek and Dude. They have other names but they're not important. You know Dodo already. Gentlemen, take the lady's coat. Show her you know how to behave in company."

He pulled off his own overcoat as he spoke, and tossed it onto an overloaded coatrack where, by a miracle, it stuck. Pud and Deek made an elaborate show of removing her wrap, and holding it between them headed toward an adjacent door into a bedroom.

"Will you excuse me a moment, Edwina?" Dude asked, his eyes fixed on her in a delighted stare. "I have to look after the stew. Sorry I'm not as good a cook as Harry."

"May I help?" she inquired, like a proper guest.

"No, no. You're company." He grinned. "Anyway, you're company tonight. I'll manage." He went out another door to a kitchenette.

The room into which Edwina had been so unceremoni-

146

ously propelled was a large one, with French windows and a big fireplace. In other days it had probably served as an upstairs parlor or music room for a private family. Now the paint was peeling off the walls and the woodwork had lost its original polish. It was furnished atrociously with huge overstuffed chairs and sofa, books and magazines strewn everywhere.

"You like it?" Harry asked, as though it was a palace.

"Very much," she said, reflecting that it did indeed have one quality which Margaret's tasteful apartment lacked —it looked lived-in.

He led her to the sofa. "Sit down and get your breath while you have a chance. What do you think of my family?"

"They are . . ." She searched for the suitable word. "They're a surprise."

Dude reappeared carrying a tray with two glasses filled with an amber liquid. "It's only cider," he explained. "Do you like cider, Edwina? Harry thinks it's the best drink for us in our situation."

"I love cider," she said, taking the proffered glass. "What is your situation, Dude?"

"We're all young men on the brink of life," he explained solemnly.

Pud and Deek dashed back and plunked themselves down on the floor in front of Edwina.

"We want to know the history of your life," Pud said.

"You tell me yours first," she countered.

"It's pretty short," Deek told her. "I was born, went to Harvard, graduated, came to New York to set it on fire. Likewise for Dude and Pud. We looked up Harry, who graduated two years before we did, so we could get some pointers. When we saw what a beautiful big apartment he had, we decided to move in with him. And here we are . . .." He was interrupted by three knocks at the door, followed by a pause and three more knocks—apparently a form of password. "Here are the girls." He scrambled to his feet and opened the door.

"Edwina is here," he announced to two attractive young women, both in slacks and plaid sport shirts.

They were called Maybelle and Etta, Edwina learned in the confusion of introductions that followed. Maybelle was an actress—at least, she made the rounds of theatrical agencies every day though her abilities were so far unappreciated. When she was tired of going to theatrical agencies, she was going to marry Pud, who by then would be earning maybe ninety dollars a week. Etta worked in a department store, selling yard goods in the drapery department. Later on, she was going to design fabrics. Deek wanted her to be engaged to him, but she had refused because of her career. Maybelle and Etta lived in the furnished apartment upstairs, which was cheaper than this one because there was one more flight of stairs to climb.

Maybelle sat down on the floor by Deek, crosslegged like a Turk. "Edwina, you're just the way Harry said you were. Why don't you come here and live with us? We've adopted Harry as our father. You could be our mother."

"Don't be silly, Maybelle," said Etta, who had curled up in an armchair. "She's no older than you are. If you adopt a mother, she has to be old enough to be your mother."

Before Edwina could comment on this, Dude popped

148

his head in the doorway. "The stew's ready. Pud and Deek —you have to serve."

"*With* pleasure," said Pud. The two of them followed Dude to the kitchenette and returned with individual trays, on each of which there was a plate of stew, a buttered roll, a fork and a paper napkin. Plates, trays, forks —all were of ten-cent-store variety and nothing matched.

Harry tested the stew. "Dude, you put onions in it," he said accusingly. "I told you Edwina might not like onions."

"You can't make stew without onions. Everyone knows that," Dude defended himself.

"I do like onions, Dude," Edwina said. "Particularly in stew."

"You do?" He beamed at her. "You see, Harry?"

"Do you know how to cook, Edwina?" Pud demanded. "We asked Harry but he said he didn't know. Maybelle knows how to cook. You should taste her scrambled eggs and bacon. What do you cook?"

Mixed as were Edwina's emotions at the calm acceptance of her as being something important in Harry's life, she was beginning to feel at home. "My mother is Norwegian," she told them. "We ate Norwegian food at home most of the time. I can make some of the dishes."

"You hear that, Harry?" demanded Deek. "Imagine anyone being able to cook Norwegian food! You should have found out about that and told us."

"What do Norwegians eat?" Maybelle wanted to know.

"Any number of things," said Edwina. "Like *Smørgoas* and *Fiskefarce* and *Kylling* and *Spekelaar*."

They howled with laughter as she pronounced each

149

strange word, and then she had to explain the ingredients of each. "Of course, my father sometimes likes steaks and chops and Yorkshire pudding," she added. "We had those at home, too."

"You hear that, Harry?" Deek repeated. "She can make steaks and chops and Yorkshire pudding. You sure are lucky."

"Edwina, may I ask you something?" Maybelle interrupted.

"Of course."

"The next time you come will you wear your yellow dress—the one that makes you look like a Dresden figurine?"

Edwina turned to Harry. "What have you been telling them? What dress?"

Harry gave her a look of guileless innocence. "Why, I suppose she means the dress you wore the first time we had lunch," he said.

"You remember, Edwina?" broke in Etta. "The time you ate at the Château Rouge when you had your hair all in curls. Harry fell in love with you then."

Discounting this last remark, Edwina still couldn't believe Harry hadn't noticed how outlandish her costume was on that first painful date.

"I put that dress in the back of my closet," she told Maybelle. "I decided it was a dreadful dress."

"I'm sure you're wrong," Maybelle said. "Next time you come, you will wear it, won't you?"

The plates were cleared, seconds were served to the men, though all three girls refused. Dude brought on a huge birthday cake with one flaming candle in the center, stating that it was nobody's birthday but he had to use up the candle somehow. Harry, as head of the household, cut the cake. Maybelle and Etta did the serving, while Dude poured coffee from a battered aluminum drip pot into cups that were either without handles or chipped at the edges.

A little questioning on Edwina's part revealed that Pud was planning to be an architect, though so far he was only a clerk in an architect's office. Deek had editorial ambitions, but was temporarily employed as a correspondent in the circulation department of a magazine. Dude was taking his Ph.D. at Columbia.

She also discovered that in spite of their seeming flippancy, Harry's "children" were concerned with many matters outside their personal interests. As they sprawled around on the floor or draped themselves on the furniture, they discussed with intensity such subjects as existentialism, San Francisco's beat generation, subliminal advertising, the struggle for integration in the South, and how to avert a third world war. Sometimes their ideas were naïve, but they were definitely their own. When Harry spoke it was usually to question a statement or a conclusion.

"We call him Socrates the Second," Pud explained to Edwina at one such interruption. "Remember how the old boy used to go around quizzing people about what they thought and making them admit things they hadn't intended to admit? Harry uses the same bag of tricks."

"Pay no attention to him," said Harry. "He's a flatterer."

Still Edwina was impressed with the real zeal, underneath all the banter, with which Harry took his respon-

151

sibility of guiding this "family" of his, only a couple of years younger than he.

"Time to go to bed," Harry announced finally, rising. "The party's over."

"Not yet." Maybelle and Etta, colliding over each other, each took one of his arms and sat him down again. "We haven't had our bedtime story."

"Not tonight," he said. "We've got company."

"Please," they coaxed.

"Well, maybe." He yielded like any indulgent parent, and his face lighted mischievously. "Tonight's episode is entitled 'Edwina and the Motion Picture Actress.'"

"Don't, Harry," Edwina begged him.

He ignored her. "Once upon a time," he began and in fairy-tale style told of the poor little motion picture actress who wept so many tears New York was in danger of being flooded, and of how three wise men (himself, the press agent and Mr. Rierdon) were summoned to find the source of the tears but proved not to be so wise after all, and how finally the fairy godmother (Edwina) arrived, how she produced a genie (Mr. Blakeley) with a magic brew (a cup of tea)—and everyone lived happily ever after.

"Tomorrow night, same time, same place," he concluded. "Get going, kids."

Maybelle and Etta with similar pouts headed for the door; Pud, Deek and Dude volunteered to escort them to their apartment—so as to protect them from highway robbers—and for a few moments Harry and Edwina were left alone.

Harry paced back and forth in front of the fireplace, his face unexpectedly troubled.

"Are you angry with me, Edwina?"

She considered the question thoughtfully. "No, I don't think so. Should I be?"

"I guess you very well could be," he said.

"I'll tell you the truth," she said. "It was the nicest evening I've had since I came to New York."

His eyes lighted up. "Do you mean that?"

She nodded.

"And Matt?"

"We were never really engaged," she said. "I thought we were sort of, but we weren't really." She looked up and saw he was laughing at her. "I mean, he decided I had too much class for him and that finished it," she ended lamely.

"Your words don't make sense but the conclusion is splendid."

He sat down beside her and took her by her shoulders. "I'm really a coward," he said. "I had to gather a whole army around me to let you know I want you to be my girl. Will you?"

"Yes," she said softly. Surprising how right everything seemed. She should have known the first day she saw him that this was what she wanted.

"Oops, sorry!" The door had opened without their noticing, and Deek, Pud and Dude were standing in front of them like three curious schoolboys.

"Think nothing of it," said Harry, not releasing her. "The future Mrs. G. Harrison Dawes has just received her first kiss."

"Hurrah!" shouted Pud, and without further ado crouched down on the floor and with a single movement

153

was standing on his head, waving his long legs wildly in the air.

While the other two were doing their best to imitate him, Harry and Edwina, like conspirators, silently sneaked away.

Chapter 13

The phone rang on Edwina's desk and she picked it up.

"Miss Fiske?"

"Yes, it is."

"This is Max Deerfield calling. Say, I'm awfully sorry I wasn't able to get to your shindig yesterday. I was tied up with Ursula Manisch, the swimming champion, at the Versailles."

"We're sorry too, Mr. Deerfield."

"I want to ask you a favor, Miss Fiske. Would you get hold of that Mike O'Hara fellow and arrange an interview for me? Make it at the factory. I want to see what sort of work he does. Human interest, you know."

"I'll see what I can do, Mr. Deerfield. He's rather publicity-shy."

"Good girl. I knew you would."

"Oh, and Mr. Deerfield, if you do that story you might mention that from now on tea is going to be served at the Rierdon factory twice a day—at eleven and at four. It was voted this morning. The people there want it, and according to statistics elsewhere the drinking of tea gives the workers a lift at the right times and actually increases production."

"I see what you mean," he said, chuckling. "I don't see why it can't be worked in. Just get me that interview."

"I'll do my best," she repeated.

She hung up the phone thoughtfully. A week ago a personal call from Max Deerfield would have made her feel she was on the top rung of the ladder to success. Now it seemed singularly unimportant.

It so happened that no South American countries had changed governments the day of the Rierdon Soap Company charity tea. There had been no developments of note in the Middle East, no spectacular controversies at the United Nations, no attempts to send rockets to the moon, no airplane crashes or Fifth Avenue jewelry robberies or juvenile delinquent outbreaks. Thus the reconciliation of a Hollywood star with her long-lost father, in itself not a world-shaking event, had received press attention far in excess of its real news value.

Edwina had already scanned the morning papers. Their tea-party incident had made all of them in one form or another, human-interest feature stories in the *Times* and *Herald Tribune,* stories up near the front in the tabloids, with more pictures than text.

All morning the phone had been ringing—requests for photographs, for special interviews and the like, calls which Pat referred to Edwina since Jeff Odell had not shown up.

One of the calls was from Harry who told her he was being similarly bombarded, the best news being that a leading business magazine wanted to do a picture story on the Rierdon factory. He did not mention the night before—he had put his business personality back on—but the tone of his voice told her all she needed to know.

For herself, she was carrying out her duties as in a dream. In her mind it seemed to her that the papers were missing the biggest scoop of all, the momentous fact that overnight the world had changed from a place of trial and struggle to a rosy paradise, where one loved and was loved in turn. What other news event could hold a candle to that miraculous circumstance?

Eric wandered into the office. "Quite a stunt you and Dawes pulled off yesterday," he said in a nasty tone of voice.

"Wasn't it?" she remarked cheerily, not bothering to inform him that Mike O'Hara's unscheduled speech had not been arranged by Harry or her.

Eric addressed Anna. "That one is getting too conceited for her own good."

"Eric, you shouldn't say that," Anna protested. "Not after all Edwina did for you."

"I'll be hearing about that from now until Doomsday," he snapped, and walked off.

To Edwina their voices were like the droning of bees.

At noon while she was at the switchboard, Dorothea told her that Mr. Odell still wasn't feeling well, that he wouldn't be in that day.

This information did penetrate her dream world, and she was horrified. The sickness was a stall, she was sure. She was positive that the blow had finally fallen, but that nobody wanted to tell her. All Thursday and Friday she handled his work as best she could. On Friday afternoon she marched into Dorothea's office, determined to learn the truth.

"How is Mr. Odell?" she demanded.

"Poor man," Dorothea said, "he's at St. Margaret's Hospital for observation. It's an old heart ailment. I hope he'll be back Monday."

He really was sick, then! Edwina was torn between relief that he hadn't been fired and concern for his welfare. She brooded about it over the weekend and on Sunday evening decided to call up the hospital and find out for herself how he was. After all, as his secretary, she had a right.

It took an interminable time to get through to him, perhaps, she reasoned, because she didn't know his room number. She was switched from one person to another until finally, when about the fifth strange voice came on the wire, she cried out in exasperation, "I'm trying to reach Mr. Jefferson Odell. Will you tell me please whether he is or isn't there?"

There followed a pause and then a woman said softly, "I'm very sorry, Mr. Odell died several hours ago."

For a long time she sat by the phone without even the strength to hang the receiver back on the hook. It was her first close contact with death and it left her stunned and shivering. A clicking on the phone made her hang up automatically. Hours later, it seemed, Harry called up to remind her she was to have dinner with him and the children. She told him the news in a low tone and begged to be excused. He offered to come over but she insisted she had to be alone. She was grateful Margaret was out of town this weekend, as she could not have faced her either.

She went into her room, closed the door and lay down,

but inaction was unbearable too. Then she did a strange thing. She got up, took from an envelope the material Dr. Rifkin had given her to prepare her first woman's club lecture on books and authors, and sat down at her typewriter. Hour after hour passed and she worked on steadily, not stopping to eat and not allowing herself to think about anything but the job at hand. Dawn came when she finally finished, and sheer exhaustion allowed her to sleep for a short time.

There is an office maxim that no one person is irreplaceable. But though Edwina was the most affected emotionally by Jeff Odell's death, the entire staff was touched deeply by it. Even Eric went around subdued and quiet for a few days, and Dorothea, guilty no doubt about her complaints of his laxness—the ones which Patricia had overheard—was loud in her protestations of grief. But work had to go on just the same. A new routine had to be set up.

A week after the funeral, Mr. Pritchard called an office meeting in the conference room. After saying what a fine person Jeff Odell had been and how much they all would miss him, he brought up the fact that the tea account still needed someone in charge of it. He had thought, he said, of bringing in someone from the outside, but on principle he was opposed to this. It was better to give a person in their own ranks a chance at it.

If he offers it to me, I will not take it, Edwina decided determinedly. It would be more than I could bear.

Every business needed new blood, he continued blandly, and it was a good thing when that new blood was young blood. There was one member of their staff who, though youthful, had proved worthy of greater responsibility. From now on Eric Kingston would be tea-account executive.

Edwina would be of inestimable aid to Eric as his secretary, he continued, since she had worked with Jeff and knew his job so well. In order that she could devote herself to helping Eric, they were hiring another young woman to do Dr. Rifkin's work.

"Aren't I the lucky one?" Eric remarked with a mocking grin as they filed out of the room.

Edwina said nothing.

She had lunch that noon with Anna, the only person now that Mr. Odell was gone who knew how unfair Mr. Pritchard's decision was.

"You're not happy about working with Eric, I can see that," Anna said over their sandwiches. "It's all my fault. If I hadn't urged you to write his stories, you would be in his place."

"That's not so," Edwina assured her. "Mr. Pritchard would never consent to a woman being one of his account executives. If it hadn't been Eric, he would have brought in someone else who might have been equally obnoxious."

"You do dislike Eric, don't you?"

"I dislike him mostly because he has taken advantage of you and made you lend him money you couldn't spare."

"Oh, what does money mean?" Anna cried out. "He needed it desperately for . . . debts of honor. I live alone in one room. I don't have to spend much. I'd rather he had it."

"You are loyal, aren't you?" Edwina said compassionately. "All right, dear, as long as I'm here I'll try to keep his head above water. More than that I cannot promise."

But it was worse than she had expected.

As soon as she came back from lunch, Eric rang for her.

It went against the grain to see him already established behind Mr. Odell's desk in the Victorian office that he had fixed up to please himself.

"Did you want something, Eric?" she asked, politely enough.

"Yes," he said curtly. "In the first place from now on you will call me Mr. Kingston. Pritchard would want it that way."

She could hardly believe he was serious. "Certainly, *Mister* Kingston," she said, as if it were a joke.

"Good." He did not meet her eyes. "Now we'll get to work. Will you kindly bring in all of the tea press books?"

There were ten in all, one for each of the ten years that Pritchard had had the account, and they were heavy. Edwina lugged them in a couple at a time and stacked them in the corner while Eric sat smoking a cigarette and pretending to be deeply absorbed in a newspaper.

"That's that," she announced on her last trip.

"Excellent." He sounded as if he were praising a youngster for filling up the woodbox. "Now will you hand me Volume One?"

It was on the bottom of the stack.

"I will not," she said and walked out.

Five minutes later he rang for her again. Volume One was on his desk.

"You win," he said. "I was just testing you."

"You'd better not test me any further," she warned him.

"All right, forget it. Listen. Five years ago we put out a story about safeguarding your own health, eating right, sleeping right, and drinking tea. I want you to mimeograph that story again and send it out to feature editors. What do you think of that?"

"I think it's stupid."

He bristled. "Why is it stupid? The editors have all changed, and if they haven't they've forgotten."

Edwina shrugged. "It's a lazy way of doing things. If we do a story on tea and health today, we should bring it up to date, get some new medical authorities to quote, and so forth. Some of the editors may have longer memories than you think. And if they don't, perhaps Mr. Blakeley will."

"That old fussbudget," Eric sneered. "He doesn't even know what day it is."

He had no sooner made this character analysis than in walked Mr. Pritchard with the tea executive in person. Eric sprang to his feet.

"Mr. Blakeley, this is Eric Kingston who is going to be your man from now on," Mr. Pritchard introduced them.

"How do you do, young man," Blakeley said. "Upset us no end about Odell. Hope you know what you're doing."

"I'll do my best, sir," Eric told him unctuously.

"And this is Miss Fiske who will be working with Eric." Mr. Pritchard gestured in Edwina's direction.

"Ah yes, Miss Fiske." Mr. Blakeley's eyes twinkled. "Delighted. Quite a show we had the other day, what?" He chuckled; then, remembering this was a visit of condolence, cut himself short. "Poor old Odell. He would have liked it."

"What did I tell you?" Eric demanded when the two

had departed. "I've met Blakeley a dozen times and he didn't even remember me."

Edwina refrained from the obvious comment that she had only met Mr. Blakeley once and he remembered her.

There was one other bright spot in that dismal day and that was just before Edwina left when Dr. Rifkin stopped her in the hallway. "I want you to know, Miss Fiske, that it was Pritchard's idea I needed a full-time secretary. For my money you can easily do as much work in half a day as the average person does in a full day."

"That's very nice of you to say, Dr. Rifkin. I'm going to miss working with you."

"Oh, we're not through yet," he assured her, tugging at his beard. "I've been meaning to tell you. You did a superb job on the woman's club lecture. I spoke to Pritchard about it, and it's decided you will do it regularly. Since it will be on your own time, you will receive extra compensation."

The piece of work she had done to escape from the shock of Mr. Odell's death—this was the one that had gained her first recognition from the boss who was opposed to women doing publicity! Something told her that Jeff would have been pleased it had worked out that way.

Chapter 14

It amazed Edwina in the weeks that followed how Mr. Pritchard could be so blind as not to see that the tea account was going steadily downhill. But then it was his nature that once he had decided Eric was a good man, he should leave him strictly on his own. He had other things to attend to—among them a new account for a large insecticide company—which occupied his energies.

Over Edwina's objections, Eric insisted on sending out the five-year-old story on tea and health. Whether the feature editors remembered it or not, it was not used. The same fate awaited several other stories that Eric resurrected from the past. One was on different ways of making iced tea, and he wouldn't listen to Edwina when she pointed out that food editors were more interested in iced tea in July than in a cold and wintry March.

With all the instruction he had received from Jeff Odell, he had no discrimination about the kind of publicity that would benefit the tea industry in America, or even of the difference between good and bad taste in publicity. He unearthed a photograph of a notorious socialite drinking tea—a woman who had been arrested on several occasions for drunken driving. He insisted this was excellent publicity and released it to the newspapers. A couple of tabloids used it, but with sarcastic captions. He also had the bright idea of persuading a gangster who was about to be executed for murder to ask for a cup of tea before he was led to the electric chair, but fortunately he was too lazy to try to see it through.

Because it was in her blood Edwina continued for a while to make suggestions of her own, but he rejected them all. He had had enough of her meddling in his work, he told her rudely. She resigned herself to doing just what he told her and no more. Under the circumstances there was nothing else she could do.

If her days at Robert Pritchard & Associates had become a painful ordeal, her outside life had plenty of compensations.

Every evening except when he had some business engagement she saw Harry. Usually they had dinner at his apartment with his "family." Edwina, no longer a guest, took over the supervision of the cooking, accomplishing wonders on the two-burner gas stove in the kitchenette. They all admitted it was an enormous improvement over the meals devised by Harry or Dude. One evening she made them a real Norwegian dinner. Neither Maybelle nor Etta were trained in culinary skills as Edwina was, but they were useful for cutting up lettuce, paring vegetables, setting the table, or any other chore Edwina assigned to them. The boys went on shifts for the dishes.

The nice thing about these evenings was that they were always fun. The disappointments of adulthood had not yet touched these young people. They had a thousand jokes they shared with each other. Even Maybelle's turn-downs at the various theatrical agencies she visited became a source of laughter when she told them to this eager and sympathetic audience.

Once Edwina brought Anna along with her. At first she was shy and stiff, but no one could long resist the antics of the boys and the warm friendliness of Maybelle and Etta, and soon she was laughing with the others. During the course of the evening, Maybelle and Etta took her upstairs to see their apartment, and when they returned they had brushed out her hair loosely, applied lipstick and a touch of rouge and eye shadow with professional skill, and adorned her in a Chinese housecoat that completed her transformation into a glamour girl.

Dude professed himself smitten and dragged her into a corner where he talked to her at great length in low tones.

"What are you telling her?" Harry demanded.

"What do you think?" said Dude. "I'm telling her about myself. She's listening, too."

The next morning at the office it was a disappointment to find that Anna had reverted to her usual drab and colorless appearance.

"Eric would have fallen in love with you if he could have seen you last night," Edwina whispered to her.

Anna shook her head. "No," she said knowingly. "He will never fall in love with me or any other woman. He likes himself too much."

She and Anna had very little chance to exchange confidences now, because of the presence of Dr. Rifkin's new secretary at the previously empty desk. She was a quiet young woman named Miss Bunting, who had a Master's in English Literature. Eric considered her a "Blue Nose" and ignored her. He rarely came into their office now anyway, for which Edwina was grateful, though she knew Anna missed his visits.

Once or twice a week Harry insisted that the two of them go out to dinner by themselves. Invariably his "family" put up a howl, claiming they wanted to go along too. But he would be firm. "Ah, no. Children are all right in their place, but sometimes grownups have to get away from them and talk about important things."

Much as Edwina was amused by Harry's home life, she was happiest on these nights alone with him. Not that they did anything special. They ate in small inexpensive restaurants—an Armenian one on Third Avenue; a French one on East 29th Street where the proprietor was the cook and his wife, a stout woman from Brittany, served as waitress; a Viennese place in the East Eighties, or a Spanish-American café in Greenwich Village. On one occasion they ventured down to Chinatown to a little basement hideout which Harry claimed served the best Chinese food in town. Another time they went uptown to Harlem to a restaurant specializing in southern fried chicken. When their dates fell on week nights, they usually sat and talked until closing time; then the nights began to get warm enough for them to take walks in the parks or along the river. Over the weekend they might go to a movie or more rarely a play.

For Edwina it was unimportant where they went or what they ate, as long as they were together.

"I never did understand why you asked me out to lunch that first time," she said one evening as they sat prolonging their coffee in the French restaurant that had become their favorite.

"Do you remember the first time we saw each other?" he countered.

"Of course. When Mr. Pritchard brought me into Jeff's office."

"No, it wasn't," he said. "It was fifteen minutes before that when I first came in. You were sitting on that turquoise sofa, looking like a stubborn wild flower. I decided then you were the sort of girl I wanted to marry—that is, when I settled down enough to marry."

She was amazed. "You noticed me then?"

"That's right. Mind you, I'm not saying I fell in love with you at first sight. I only decided I wanted to marry someone like you."

Sometimes it was hard to tell whether Harry was joking or serious.

"I thought you were in love with Millicent Madden," she confided.

"You did?" He pursed his lips thoughtfully. "That gives me an idea. Let's go call on her."

A few minutes' walk brought them to the charming apartment just off Gramercy Park where Millicent Madden lived—with her husband, Dr. Neville, a heart specialist, a teen-age daughter and an eight-year-old son. They had a lovely evening, during which Millicent talked to Edwina about her children's schooling while the doctor engaged Harry in a discussion of the political situation in the Far East.

"Do you still think I should fall in love with Millicent?" Harry demanded on their way home.

"But people always call her Miss Madden. How was I to know?"

"Many women in business keep their maiden names

after marriage," he said. "That way if they get divorced and take a new husband, they have no problem of explaining another change of names to their business associates."

"A gruesome idea," she said, wrinkling up her nose at him. "Let's not think about it."

Margaret had accepted the news of Edwina's engagement with what Edwina recognized as relief. In spite of Margaret's hospitality, she felt herself a disturbing element in her aunt's life. Margaret was too used to living alone to want her niece as a permanent boarder. Once Edwina brought Harry to dinner on an evening when Dr. Rifkin was also a guest. He put on his business personality for the occasion, including his glasses and most expensive suit, and it delighted Edwina when Margaret said afterwards that Harry seemed like a fine sort of person, "but perhaps a little too old and serious for you, my dear."

She had written to her family about him too, and while they regretted they couldn't meet "her young man" beforehand, they were happily planning to come to New York for the wedding.

They planned this tentatively for September, by which time Harry figured he would have been able to pay off most of the debts incurred for his younger brother's education and they could start with a clean slate in their own apartment.

"It won't be very elegant," he warned her. "Not at first."

"We'll get ourselves a chicken coop," Edwina suggested. "Then one day we'll cast a magic spell and turn it into a castle."

About her difficulties at the office she said as little as possible. There seemed no way of altering the situation at the present, and she knew anything she might say to Harry would only make him unhappy.

One day he called her at the office. "Can you meet me for lunch right away?"

"Why, yes." Eric had been closeted with Mr. Pritchard all morning and had thus had no opportunity to load her down with all the futile harassing chores he usually thought up to keep her busy.

They met in the Italian restaurant where they had lunched so many times as casual friends. As soon as he had ordered, Harry said, "Edwina, it looks as though the magic spell you talked about has been cast."

"What do you mean?" She could tell he was excited.

"This," he said. "The Tea Conference Board has just informed Pritchard that their contract is being canceled as of the end of the month. It seems your Eric Kingston has been up to some stunts that weren't very ethical—I don't know what, but they're through."

That explained Eric's being in the president's office all morning.

"Poor Eric," she said impulsively, "I feel sorry for him. He'll be out of a job."

"What a way to react!" he commented. "Why don't you think of yourself for a change?"

"Why, I'll be out of a job too." The thought was almost pleasant.

"Let me go on," he told her. "Mr. Blakeley has been over at my office this morning. They want us to take on the tea account."

"Oh, Harry, that's wonderful news!" She knew that one large industrial account like this would likely bring in more than most of their other clients combined. It meant success for Madden and Dawes.

"Wait a minute before you congratulate me. He made one condition." Harry's face was impassive. "His condition was that when we take over the account, we should take you over too—to handle it under Millicent's and my supervision."

She stared at him incredulously. "I will be working for you—with you?"

"It's pretty awful, isn't it?" He grinned at her. "Think twice before you speak, Edwina. If you say yes, you'll have to sit across from me at breakfast, listen to me all day long, and cook my dinner for me at night. Nobody should ask that much of anybody."

"I think I can stand it," Edwina said finally.

Chapter 15

Madden and Dawes was like an army barrack compared to the elegance of Robert Pritchard & Associates. Millicent and Harry had been much too busy in their first year of business to worry about interior decoration. The two rooms of their offices were bare and functional, their plainness relieved only by a coat of cheery yellow paint. Furniture was secondhand and typewriters renovated.

A young man named Billy, a friend of Pud's, answered the phone in the outside room, relaying messages to the inner office by buttons and buzzers. In the same room Mrs. Markowitz had her desk. She was an elderly woman, hired for efficiency rather than glamour, who took dictation. Millicent and Harry shared the inner room, their desks face to face. When one of them was out, Edwina could sit at the empty desk. Otherwise she got along with a typewriter table next to Billy. She had been there a week and was so radiantly happy that the makeshift accommodations didn't bother her in the slightest.

Both Millicent and Harry were out on this morning. They had gone to the Tea Conference Board for the purpose of signing the contract. Edwina had settled herself at Harry's desk to work on the assignment that Millicent had given her.

It was preparing a story on Trilbies, the line of low-heeled "high-style" shoes designed by Millicent's new client, for the beauty editor of *Chic* magazine. Millicent had sold the beauty editor on the idea of the story—about the importance of a graceful walk in creating an impression of beauty—over a lunch at Longchamps. But she was only too happy to turn the actual writing over to Edwina. Millicent preferred the part of publicity involving talking with people and creating story ideas; writing was drudgery to her. They thus supplemented each other perfectly, for Edwina still felt herself too inexperienced to enjoy the strain of meetings with the press. That could come later.

After a few false starts she had decided to build the story from the line in one of Byron's poems, "She walks in beauty like the night." It would stress that the first impression a charming woman makes is by the way she moves. It would go on to show that women walk better in comfortable shoes than on spike heels—and that the advantage of Trilbies was that they were both handsome and comfortable. When she had finished it to her satisfaction she put the draft on Millicent's desk.

In one week's time her life at Robert Pritchard & Associates had become as unreal as a mirage. Edwina had given notice to Mr. Pritchard the afternoon after she lunched with Harry. Though she had offered to stay the week out, Mr. Pritchard had said that wouldn't be necessary. Her one desire was to get away quickly. She had made rather tearful farewells to Anna and Pat and even

Dorothea, but she hadn't seen Eric before she left. She still didn't know what had happened to him.

How little it seemed to matter now!

The important thing was to build up Madden and Dawes so that they would one day be the biggest and best publicity agency in New York. She put her elbows on Harry's desk and her head on her hands, daydreaming about an office so stunning it would put Pritchard's to shame. They could not stop with the tea account. They had to have others just as good. While she was waiting for Harry and Millicent to return, she decided to get to work on it.

She picked up the phone and dialed Matt's business number.

"Matt, this is Edwina."

"Hello there," he said. "This is a surprise. How's the career girl?"

"Still being a career girl," she said. "This call is strictly business." She told him about her present job.

"Splendid," he congratulated her. "I suppose you want to start by getting a new account?"

"You guessed it right off," she admitted.

"The truth is, you picked a good time," he told her. "We're just establishing a system which will make it possible for us to handle a great deal more business. As a matter of fact, Mr. Blanchard was saying just this morning he'd like to find a reputable firm to do some publicity for us."

"My goodness, I'm glad I happened to call! Can you set up a luncheon and have him meet my boss?"

"Certainly. I'll call you back when I've had a chance to check with him. Anything else I can do for you?"

"Not a thing," she told him.

She hung up with the feeling that one reason Matt was so co-operative was that she had been proved right: that there was another girl now, or perhaps a second and a third, and that in his curious fashion he felt guilty about her. Well, it would do no harm to let him go on feeling guilty—at least until Harry had a chance to talk with Mr. Blanchard.

She looked up to see Millicent storming into the room like a small cyclone.

"Millicent, I think I may have a new account for us," Edwina burst out. "It's an old friend of mine. Harry suggested it originally. We're arranging a lunch together . . ." She stopped short, seeing Millicent's face a mask of tragedy. "Is something the matter?"

"Something utterly, utterly horrible has happened." Millicent threw her gloves and her bag on her desk and plopped herself down dramatically. "The Tea Conference Board will not sign the contract."

"What?" Edwina stared at her incredulously. "Why won't they? I thought it was all settled."

"It was." Millicent threw out her hands in a gesture of complete despair. "We had a gentlemen's agreement with them, which in the trade is considered as binding as a contract. But they've changed their minds. They won't have anything to do with us."

"Please be specific, Millicent," Edwina pleaded. "Tell me exactly what happened."

"They think we're connivers, that we planned everything, that we resorted to underhanded methods—I don't know what all." Her eyes flashed with anger. "It's the most ridiculous thing I ever heard in my life."

175

"Millicent, what are their exact charges?" Edwina could not make heads or tails out of all this tirade.

She shrugged. "Oh, they say that we put you up to deliberately sabotaging Eric Kingston's work—so that we could get the account for ourselves. Did you ever hear anything so *insane?* Why, we didn't even know what was going on there until Blakeley came to Harry and asked him to take over the account."

"What do they mean about my sabotaging the account?" Edwina demanded with icy coolness. "What do you mean about what was going on there?"

"Oh, you know—about your allegedly sending out stories that were no good without young Kingston's knowledge . . . copying a story used in the *Register* for a *Globe* editor."

"Mr. Blakeley says I did that?" Edwina could not believe her ears. "I thought Mr. Blakeley liked me."

"He did. That's one of the grievances. He says that an Eton schoolmaster once told him never to trust a woman with a pretty face. That's you. He says he's learned his lesson."

"Didn't you tell him none of it was true?"

"Try reasoning with a stubborn Englishman," Millicent sighed, throwing up her hands so that her charm bracelets jingled. "The facts are all there against you."

"Millicent, what facts? You still haven't told me."

"What does it matter? It's too late now. Something about a feature story in the *Register* with Tony Burke's by-line. *Diet Habits of Athletes* or something like that."

"Tea Heads Beverage List of Athletes," Edwina corrected her automatically. "I took the call when Mr. Burke called up and asked for some help on the story. He had

been interviewing boxers and track stars and a lot of other athletes to find out their preferred drink, and found that when they're in training many of them drink tea. He wanted information about tea's nutritional value. I told him about Riboflavin, which supplies Vitamin B. But that story appeared months ago. What has that got to do with me?"

Millicent looked over at her bleakly. "You don't know that the same story was sent to Nat Folsom of the *Globe* a couple of weeks or so ago as an exclusive? Well, it seems it was. Nat just happened to recognize it and was so furious he called up the Tea Conference Board people. That was the main reason Pritchard lost the account."

Edwina shook her head, dumfounded. "I can't believe even Eric would be stupid enough to do that. Why, it's the worst crime a publicity man can commit!"

"You didn't do it, did you?"

That she should even be questioned about such a fantastic charge was a wound. "Do you and Harry *think* I did it?"

"No, of course not, darling," Millicent assured her. "I just wanted to hear you say it."

But the poison was there. It was dreadful enough to have Mr. Blakeley suspect her, that he would believe whatever Eric might have made up about her. But if Harry had even the slightest doubts about her innocence she felt she could never bear to see him again.

"Where is Harry now, Millicent?" she asked, with a cold premonition.

"He said he had some things to do. Maybe he just couldn't bear to bring you the bad news."

"All right," said Edwina dully. "Since he isn't here I'll

see what I can do about it." She picked up the phone, dialed Pritchard, and asked for Anna.

"It's nice of you to call," she heard Anna's voice. "We were such good friends, weren't we, Edwina? But some things have happened . . . I don't understand . . . I'm sorry, but I don't think I can make lunch today."

"Anna, please. It's very important. Please drop whatever else you have to do and meet me in the lunchroom at twelve o'clock."

"Well, all right. . . ." Anna's voice trailed off doubtfully.

If Anna was the poorest liar in the world, she also was frank. No sooner were they in a booth opposite to each other than she said, "I want you to know I don't blame you, Edwina."

"Anna, you don't believe I planted that Tony Burke story?" Edwina cried out.

"Eric says you did," Anna said. "Of course, I knew you were in love with Mr. Dawes and that a woman will do almost anything for the man she loves."

"You're talking absolute nonsense, Anna! If there's one thing I could have done to hurt Harry, it would have been a stunt like that."

But reason, common sense, logic were no weapons against Anna's conviction that Edwina had done whatever she had done for love. Edwina returned to the office of Madden and Dawes in a mood of complete dejection.

Harry was not back. Millicent was off getting some color shots of a new consignment of Swedish glass. She had left a note for Edwina: "Good work on the Walk in Beauty story." This pat on the head when everything was crumbling seemed incomprehensible.

Billy buzzed the double ring that meant a call for her. She seized the phone, hoping against hope it would be Harry, calling to say he believed in her.

It was Matt to say that his Mr. Blanchard would be glad to have lunch with them the following Tuesday.

She checked through Harry's calendar. "Mr. Dawes isn't in just now, Matt," she said in a flat voice, "but he seems to be free Tuesday. I'll make a note of it for him."

"What's the matter, baby? Aren't you pleased?" he demanded.

"Certainly I am." She forced herself to sound convincing. "It's wonderful."

She spent the rest of the afternoon composing a memo to Harry about the Blanchard firm and outlining her ideas to publicize it. She felt she was writing her swan song.

That night she had dinner with Margaret, a cheese soufflé her aunt had whipped up for them when she found that Edwina wasn't going out.

Edwina couldn't touch it.

"I might as well tell you, Margaret," she said, putting down her fork, "I'm not marrying Harry Dawes after all. I've decided I've had enough of New York. I'm going home."

"What a pity," Margaret commented. "I do feel badly about it, Edwina. I've had a feeling that in all your running around you've missed so many of the treasures New York has to offer—the Metropolitan and the Museum of Natural History."

Edwina stared gloomily at the soufflé. Maybe Margaret was right. The paintings at the Metropolitan, the stuffed animals at the Museum—they would never hurt her as human beings did.

179

The next morning she stayed in bed until Margaret had left for her job. Then she got up, forced herself to drink some coffee, and began to pack. At ten o'clock the phone rang, but she did not answer. If it were the office of Madden and Dawes, if it were Harry himself, it was too late now. There was nothing more to be said. At ten-thirty the phone rang again and again she did not answer, though she found herself tempted to do so.

As soon as it stopped ringing she sat down and dialed several airline companies. One of them informed her she could have a reservation as far as Chicago if she would be at the office by one o'clock to pick up her ticket. That gave her time to go to her bank and take out her savings to pay her fare. She was determined now, and it was easy not to answer the phone when it rang, loud and long, for the third time. Instead she dressed carefully in a new sea-green summer frock, which she had been saving to wear to celebrate the signing of the tea contract.

She was lugging two suitcases from her bedroom as the front door opened. There stood Harry and Margaret.

"I told you she was perfectly all right, Mr. Dawes," Margaret said. "Just a slight indisposition."

Harry's eyes wandered from Edwina to her suitcases.

"All right?" he echoed. "Edwina, I've been calling you all morning. I finally went to your aunt's office and made her come up here with me. What on earth are you up to?"

She wanted to run into his arms. Instead she said calmly, almost lightly, "Didn't Margaret tell you? I've decided to go back to Dantonville. In view of everything, it seemed the only thing to do."

"What do you mean, in view of everything?" he demanded almost angrily. "You mean because I didn't call you last night? I couldn't. I was in the midst of some very important detective work."

"I'm not talking about your calling me or not calling me," she said, making her voice sound indifferent. "But when I ruin the reputation of Madden and Dawes, it's time for me to get away."

"What are you talking about? You don't mean that little fracas over at the Tea Conference Board?" And as she still looked at him stonily, a light seemed to dawn on him. "Millicent! I should have known. She built a mole-hill into a mountain, didn't she? Didn't I ever tell you that Millicent's one great failing is a weakness for high melo-drama? What a fool I was to let her go back to the office alone!"

And then he was holding her very tight while she burst into uncontrollable sobs.

"Pull yourself together, darling," he whispered, tugging softly at her hair. "We've got an appointment with Robert Pritchard and we're late now."

Before Margaret's startled gaze, he picked her up and carried her out the door.

"Mr. Dawes," she protested. "Nothing is ever decided by violent action."

But they were already halfway down the stairs.

Chapter 16

Mr. Pritchard's office was exactly the same as when she had first entered it except that the philodendron plants had grown a little higher. It struck Edwina as incongruous that this should be so, that the office somehow ought to reflect the different circumstances of her presence there.

Eric, Dorothea, Anna and Mr. Blakeley were seated facing Mr. Pritchard behind his desk. As Edwina and Harry made their appearance, he called out genially, "So you finally located her, Dawes. Well, pull up a couple of chairs next to me."

When they had done so, he rose and cleared his throat, just as Edwina had seen him do at that first conference many months before.

"One of the most important assets in business is a sense of fair play," he said. "A sense of fair play is as important to the losers as to the winners. In this case I have been the loser but I couldn't respect myself unless I saw that justice was done."

Dorothea was taking notes. Was she taking down every word that was said? Edwina wondered.

"Anna." Mr. Pritchard turned to the bookkeeper. "Will you repeat what you told me earlier this morning when I called you in?"

"Yes, Mr. Pritchard, I will." Anna looked not at the president but at Eric in a manner that seemed almost regal. "I told you that I had lunch with Edwina yesterday and she told me she didn't do the things Eric Kingston told you and Mr. Blakeley she had done. I didn't believe her but I want you to know that even thinking that all the things Eric said were true, I didn't blame her. She wrote those stories about the Golden Arrow Bus Lines because I begged her to, and she didn't get any credit for it. When Eric was made her boss, she had a right not to like it. And then she was going to marry Mr. Dawes so she naturally wanted to do things for him. So I didn't believe her but I didn't blame her."

"All right, all right," said Mr. Pritchard impatiently. "You didn't believe her but you didn't blame her. What happened next?"

"I went back to the office and I started thinking," continued Anna. "One thing Eric—Mr. Kingston—said Edwina had done was to send out releases to the mimeograph company without his knowing about it. I could check on that. Every release we send to be mimeographed has the initials on it of the person authorizing the order. It's an office rule, Mr. Pritchard. You made it yourself."

"I know," he urged her. "Go on."

"I called the mimeograph company and asked them to send back by messenger all the sample releases we had sent to them since Mr. Kingston took over. You must believe I don't usually order a messenger unless I am told to." She looked guiltily at Mr. Pritchard.

183

"That's all right, Anna," he said with an attempt to hide exasperation. "I think your extravagance was warranted. Please get to the point."

"I'm glad you feel that way, Mr. Pritchard. Because I thought it was important. When I got the sample releases back, I saw they all had Mr. Kingston's initials on them. He had lied about that."

Eric started, seemed about to say something, then sat back moodily.

"I realized if he lied about that he would lie about other things," Anna continued imperturbably, her eyes again fixed on Eric. "And then I remembered. He had given me a big thick letter to Nat Folsom at the *Globe* to mail for him one evening after Edwina had gone home. I remembered it because he had spelled Mr. Folsom's name with two 'l's' instead of one. Mr. Odell always said we must never misspell an editor's name. So I typed a new envelope for him."

"Did you look at the contents of the envelope when you removed them, Anna?" Mr. Pritchard asked.

"No, sir, but it was several sheets of legal-sized paper folded together. I won't say it was Mr. Tony Burke's story about athletes drinking tea which I had typed out for Eric a few days before, but I can say it might have been because it was on the same sort of paper. I can't say it was because I didn't look. But I do know that Edwina would not have spelled Mr. Folsom's name with two 'l's.' "

"Now, Eric, what have you to say to this?" Mr. Pritchard demanded, swinging his chair around to face that young man directly.

At this moment Edwina felt Harry nudge her. She

184

turned to look at him, but his eyes were fixed straight ahead over the heads of the others at the doorway to Dorothea's office, visible only to them and Mr. Pritchard from where they were sitting. In the doorway a man was standing, a middle-aged man with thin gray hair and rimless glasses, whom she had never seen before.

"Well?" Pritchard was waiting for Eric's answer.

Edwina hadn't expected Eric to break down and make a confession, but she was still unprepared for his air of aggrieved innocence.

"What can I say, sir? I don't want to make any accusations, but everyone knows it isn't difficult to forge initials —especially not for a man's own secretary. I am sure you have too much sense to take seriously this rigmarole about how Nat Folsom's name was spelled on an alleged envelope that went into the trash weeks ago."

"Oh, I didn't throw it into the wastebasket," Anna spoke up. "I saved it. It was in the back of my desk. I found it just before I came in here, Mr. Pritchard, but I didn't have a chance to tell you. Here it is."

She handed him a long envelope which she had been clutching. "You will see that Mr. Folsom's name is spelled incorrectly."

Mr. Pritchard studied the envelope. "Now what do you say, Eric?"

"The story gets sillier and sillier," Eric burst out, with considerably less self-control. "There's no proof that the envelope wasn't typed yesterday—or this morning."

Mr. Pritchard was still looking at the envelope. "Unfortunately for you, Eric, there *is* proof. This envelope went through our stamp machine three weeks ago—just

185

when Anna said it was mailed out. We seem to have the evidence well in hand. Anna, whatever made you save this?"

"I can explain that, Mr. Pritchard." Dorothea looked up from her voluminous notes. "I told Anna once to save any envelopes that were stamped and not mailed, as I thought we might get the money back from the post office."

Edwina nearly choked on this. She and the others had always felt Dorothea carried her loyalty to the company to an extreme. But because she had hoped to save the company an eight-cent stamp, Eric's lie was exposed!

"Well, Eric?" Mr. Pritchard asked for the third time.

"I say it's a frame-up!" he shouted. His face was twisted with fury now. "Everyone in the office knows how Anna Dombrowski pursued me. Because I finally had to make it clear to her she was making a nuisance of herself, she pulls something like this. She was in it with Edwina Fiske, all right."

Edwina felt Harry stiffen at her side and his fist clench. Before he could intervene, Anna cried out.

"That's not so and you know it's not, Eric! All I did was cover up for you when you said you were going out with editors and took girls to bars instead! And I paid your debts! I never asked you to take me out. I never asked you for a thing. It didn't matter what you did to me. But when I found out what you were trying to do to Edwina, that did matter! You're just no good, Eric, no good." She collapsed into sobs.

"There was never a truer word spoken, young lady."

The voice that uttered these words was icy and calm.

It came from the man with the rimless eyeglasses standing in the doorway. The others turned and stared at him.

"Mr. Kingston!" exclaimed Dorothea. And almost simultaneously, Eric ejaculated one horrified word: "Father!"

Leo Kingston, the publisher of *Fact,* Eric's father! It was clear now. Harry reached over, grasped Edwina's hand and held it tight. No one noticed.

"I'm sorry I had to let you in on this, Leo," Mr. Pritchard said.

"Glad you did, Bob," the other replied. "Eric, you will now tell these people that all the charges this young woman has so bravely brought up are true—as I know they are, since I know you."

"I . . . I . . ." Eric stuttered.

"Go on. I am waiting."

"They are true," Eric muttered, his face scarlet.

"That's that," his father said briskly. "I don't know what I'm going to do with you, but I'm sure of one thing. I won't inflict you on my friends again. Come on home, Eric."

He turned to Edwina. "I apologize for my son, Miss Fiske. I will try to make up to you and Miss Anna for what you have gone through."

When the two of them were gone, it seemed to Edwina that pandemonium broke out in the office, but actually it was only Mr. Blakeley, Mr. Pritchard, and Harry talking at once. Mr. Blakeley was telling Harry that they would sign the tea contract that afternoon, and telling Edwina he should never have trusted an embittered bachelor Eton schoolmaster. Harry was telling Mr. Pritchard that he was to be congratulated: the head of a publicity firm who would go out of his way to see that justice was done even at his own cost was making publicity history. Mr. Pritchard was saying it was nothing at all; his own blindness had caused them to lose the tea account, and he wished Madden and Dawes luck with it.

"And perhaps I'm wrong about another thing, Edwina," he added with a curious sparkle in his eyes. "Perhaps women do have a place in publicity—some women, that is, if they don't try to overstep themselves."

"I'll try never to do that, Mr. Pritchard," Edwina promised. She got up, moved over to Anna and put her arms around her. "Don't feel too upset, dear, please."

Anna looked up at her with eyes starry from her recent tears. "Why, there's nothing wrong now. I'm well again."

Harry and Edwina stepped out of the turmoil of the president's office into the serenity of the reception room.

Patricia at her desk looked up and smiled. "Is everything all right with you two now?"

"Everything," Edwina told her.

She glanced up at Abraham Lincoln, still above Patricia's desk. It seemed to her that his expression had changed since her first visit, and that he was now more tolerant of the modern decor.

Then she and Harry were out on the street in the bright July sunshine, smiling at each other.

"Where were you last night?" she challenged him.

"Three guesses," he said.

"I only need one," she told him. "Leo Kingston. Perhaps Mr. Pritchard too."

"Now I'll ask you a question," he said. "Do you know what day it is?"

188

"It's Thursday."

"Dead wrong," he said. "Today is our anniversary. One year ago today you applied for work at Pritchard's, and I saw you. Tonight we're going out for a big celebration."

"Yes, Harry, that will be fine," she said docilely. She added: "That is, if the children don't mind."